DOCTOR'S FAMILY MADE IN SICILY

LUANA DAROSA

MEDICAL ROMANCE

Recycling programs for this product may not exist in your area.

ISBN-13: 978-1-335-99379-3

Doctor's Family Made in Sicily

For questions and comments about the quality of this book, please contact us at CustomerService@Harlequin.com.

Harlequin Enterprises ULC
22 Adelaide St. West, 41st Floor
Toronto, Ontario M5H 4E3, Canada
www.Harlequin.com

HarperCollins Publishers
Macken House, 39/40 Mayor Street Upper,
Dublin 1, D01 C9W8, Ireland
www.HarperCollins.com

Printed in U.S.A.

1 2 3 4 5 6 7 8 9 10 HDC 28 27 26 25

"Hungarian legislation only permits an out-of-country adoption into a two-parent household and only after some rigorous checks. They're not willing to consider my application because I would be—*I am*—a single parent. So...they're asking me to surrender Luca to the authorities and have him returned to Hungary."

"There has to be something we can do," Layla says. "Is there anything I can do to help?"

Of course she'd want to help, but I shake my head again even before she's done speaking. "Showing up with a wife and a genuine marriage certificate is the only way my lawyer thinks we can win the goodwill of the adoption authorities in Hungary."

The time frame in which I need to deliver this marriage certificate is too short for any genuine romance. And I don't have the desire for anything real—or fake, if I'm being honest.

Her eyes flitter back to me, and when our gazes clash, some weird premonition hits me where I somehow know what she's about to say, but even so, I'm blindsided when she says, "Okay, I'll do it, then. Let's get married."

Dear Reader,

When I first sat down to write *Doctor's Family Made in Sicily*, I knew I wanted to explore two things close to my heart: the pull of family—both the ones we're born into and the ones we choose—and the courage it takes to risk your heart again after loss. I'm such a sucker for people finding love again. I can't help but make it part of their story.

Marina and Layla came to me as opposites: one rooted in her Sicilian hometown, the other a wanderer shaped by the humanitarian front lines. What surprised me was how quickly they revealed the tenderness beneath their armor, especially around their need to become a family and figure out what's best for Luca. Found family is such a personal thing for me, living with the people I call my family every day. So it was such an emotional ride to explore it on the page.

I hope Marina and Layla's journey touches you as much as it did me, and that you root for them to become the family they deserve to be.

Luana <3

Once at home in sunny Brazil, **Luana DaRosa** has since lived on three different continents, though her favorite romantic location remains the tropical places of Latin America. When she's not typing away at her latest romance novel or reading about love, Luana is either crocheting, buying yarn she doesn't need or chasing her bunnies around her house. She lives with her partner in a cozy town in the south of England. Find her on X under the handle @ludarosabooks.

Books by Luana DaRosa

Harlequin Medical Romance

Amazon River Vets

The Vet's Convenient Bride
The Secret She Kept from Dr. Delgado

Buenos Aires Docs

Surgeon's Brooding Brazilian Rival

Valentine Flings

Hot Nights with the Arctic Doc

Her Secret Rio Baby
Falling Again for the Brazilian Doc
A Therapy Pup to Reunite Them
Pregnancy Surprise with the Greek Surgeon
Falling for Her Miami Rival
Faking It with the Doctor Prince
Falling for the GP Next Door
Off-Limits Doc on Deck

Visit the Author Profile page at Harlequin.com.

For Sheila, thanks for believing in me

CHAPTER ONE

Marina

'THEY WANT TO do *what*?' I pull the phone from my ear to look at it, believing my signal must have dropped. There's no way—

'He's undocumented, Marina.' Nope, apparently my hearing is fine, and so is my signal.

'Okay, but he's *four*. There's no way they will deport a child, undocumented or not. Surely the people in Geneva have something to say about that.' My heart beats in my throat, and I'm fighting down the anxiety bubbling up in my chest. It has been a constant companion for the last six months, ever since Agron's car crash that left me looking after his son, Luca.

Giuseppe, one of my oldest friends and a family lawyer by trade, lets out a sigh. 'I don't know what to tell you. As far as procedure is concerned, they are doing exactly as expected. Regardless of what Agron told you or how you guys lived together, he was technically here illegally, and so is his son.'

'There's no way a child can be illegal, Pepe.' I say it more out of frustration than anything else. I know he's right, but that doesn't make the situation any easier to deal with. *Goddamn it, Agron. Why didn't you tell me sooner? We could have worked it out.*

I push the thought aside because thinking about him will only worsen the pressure already building in my chest, and I need to focus on Luca right now. He's someone I can still save.

I continue, 'The authorities were more than happy to leave Luca in my care since the accident. Clearly, they're not that worried about his whereabouts. And if I adopt him, then all of this will be moot. He can become an Italian citizen through me.' Like, the answer is so obvious. Why aren't the pencil pushers from the government getting on board with that?

'I've spoken to the social workers and lawyers over there. Processing a foster claim for an undocumented child of a foreign nationality is easier said than done. They have to negotiate with the other government, and that's where the difficulty is coming in,' Giuseppe says, and I hear him shuffling some papers around as if he's inspecting the correspondence sent between his office and the Italian family court.

‘So…it’s the Albanian government holding us up?’ Each vertebra cracks when I sit up straight, my back muscles protesting. I don’t know how long I’ve sat here hunched over like a shrimp, but my body is not enjoying it.

‘That’s what I’m gathering from my contacts at the family office. They say the Albanians have some…ideas of what the ideal family unit looks like. They will only approve a two-parent adoption or deport him back to Albania.’ Giuseppe sounds pained. Or maybe that’s me projecting the anguish pumping through my veins onto him.

There’s no way I’m handing Luca over to the authorities. I’d rather risk my own safety and reputation than let them take him to a country he hasn’t spent more than six months in when he has a perfectly fine home here with me. When Agron had first arrived here at my clinic four years ago looking for work, I didn’t think much about it. Running a free clinic on the southern tip of Sicily, I see refugees arrive every day—live with them in my daily life.

I’ve learned since I settled down here not to ask too many questions. As long as I have all the information I need to treat someone, I don’t concern myself with their background or history.

But Agron stuck around the clinic, and his son Luca instantly weaselled himself into my heart. When Agron told me he wasn’t a refugee but actually a paramedic from Albania looking for work, we figured something out. As a free clinic, my funds have always been limited, and whenever help comes my way I don't reject it. So I let him and his son move into my spare bedroom, which I keep for the occasional staff member that needs a place to stay before they establish themselves—or leave—and we became close friends from that moment on.

Never more than that. Even if I were attracted to men—which I'm not—I learned the lesson of not getting involved with co-workers the hard way.

The current occupant of my spare room pops into my thoughts before I can fend her off. Layla Sabri, a junior doctor currently working for the NGO under which I operate my clinic, is becoming a frequent guest in my mind against my will. Which isn't ideal, seeing how the 'no dating in the workplace' rule is firmer than ever now that I have the responsibility of Luca. Sure, for everyone in *Grey's Anatomy* the romances always worked out great, but they don't live in the real world like the rest of us.

People are far too keen to screw you over, especially when the power balance is unequal. I'm not about that kind of life.

'He doesn't even have a family in Albania.

How can they think it's better for him to live in an orphanage than here with me, where he is cared for and loved? He speaks more Italian than Albanian.' Why would the state even want an orphaned child when someone is volunteering to take care of him? 'How do we solve this? Do I have to go to Rome and speak to the Albanian ambassador to make my case?'

Giuseppe goes quiet again, which hasn't been a good sign in any of the daily conversations we have about this. 'The rules are archaic and people might be questioning them, but no one is going to change them for one case. I'll see if I can get in touch with the embassy again, but don't get your hopes up. If you don't turn up with a spouse, I don't think they will be moved to do anything.'

I swallow a frustrated groan, eyes roaming over the tiny desk I have stuffed in my bedroom to do all the admin work for the clinic. A photo of Luca and Agron sits next to my monitor, and a lump builds in my throat as I look at it. He trusted me with his son early on, and even though I never thought about children before, now I can't imagine my life without this little boy in it. There's nothing I wouldn't do for him.

'Does it matter how old the marriage certificate is?' I ask, not sure why. I don't have a plan, but I can't make one if I don't have all the information.

The rustling of paper comes through the phone again. Then Giuseppe asks, 'What are you thinking?'

'I'm saying, what if my girlfriend is willing to marry me so we can get it sorted? Would they accept that?' I don't have a girlfriend—haven't had one since I arrived in Sicily six years ago. I'm just hoping Giuseppe doesn't remember—

'You don't have a girlfriend, Marina.' Damn it. We might not see each other much since I moved away from Milan, but Giuseppe is still one of my oldest friends.

'You don't know everything,' I say, far too defensive, but I can't help it where Luca is concerned. 'Things are new, and you know I don't like talking about things after what happened with Francesca.'

The name squeezes through my tight vocal cords, and I fight down the shiver. Even that dark episode of my life led to a good outcome. It helped me fund this clinic—where I met Agron and Luca.

'Right. So, you want to marry your new girlfriend. She's on board with that?'

'I haven't asked her, but I think she might be. She loves Luca.' A picture of Layla pops into my head again, unbidden—the curve of her mouth when she's trying not to laugh, the faint scar on her wrist she hides under her watch. It's ridiculous that I even notice these things, but lately, I seem to notice everything about her.

She arrived a month ago for a six-month placement with New Health Frontier, the NGO placing doctors in clinics like my own to help vulnerable populations and make medicine more accessible.

Because the premises of my clinic are tiny, the extra staff New Health Frontier assigns me stay with me. Layla is the first person to arrive since Agron's death, and naturally that meant contact with Luca as well, whom I simply introduced as my son.

They connected instantly, like two peas in a pod, and I think it must be something Luca does to people. He charms his way even through the thickest walls.

Only problem is Layla isn't my girlfriend. She's not even my *friend*. No, she's a doctor I work with who happens to live in my apartment above my free clinic, and she gets along with my son.

My son.

That's what I'm trying to achieve here. To get a piece of paper that will let the world know what I already know to be true in my heart.

Giuseppe sighs. Even with this much water and land mass dividing us, he can tell I'm not completely honest. But he gives me the answer I need. 'The guidance I received says nothing about the minimum length of marriage. All it says is that only two-parent households are eligible to go through the evaluation process.'

'Okay, that's great. Send me the details of what the evaluation process looks like, and I will talk to…my girl about this idea.' I cringe when I stumble over my words, and I deserve the world-weary sigh I hear from Giuseppe.

'Marina—'

'Don't worry about this. Just get me the info, and I will get you the marriage certificate, okay?'

Giuseppe promises he will send things through, and when we say our goodbyes and I put the phone down I slump back in my seat, head hitting the backrest. The tension eases out of my body. Not because I'm less worried but because it's been going on for so long, my muscles are too fatigued to keep on tensing.

There is hope. It's small, and I don't know where I'm going to find a wife in the next few days—or how to stop my mind from conjuring one particular face every time I think about it—but if that's what it takes, then I'm going to do it.

Anything to keep Luca with me.

CHAPTER TWO

Layla

I HATE THE fluorescent light in the supply closet. There's nothing quite as soul-flaying as inventorying IV bags in this space, which resembles a tomb lit for autopsies. No music, no air, just the tick-tick of the electric meter inside the wall and me, counting the off-brand saline bags and cursing the New Health Frontier executives for sending me here. If I had wanted to spend my days doing mostly inventory and writing up proposals for the government to ask for funds, I could have stayed in Algiers working for a family clinic like my father wanted for me.

But how could I have stayed there when I have eyes and ears to observe the state our world is in and know I have the skills to help? That's why I signed up with New Health Frontier the moment my training was over, the need to be in a place that mattered overwhelming.

I was there months ago, working on the outskirts of a conflict zone and saving lives. Well, as many as one can with war and famine raging. The hours were gruelling and the work never-ending. But what kept me going was every single life I saved, knowing I was where I was needed most. Until I failed to save a specific life and it plunged my life into chaos.

Not that I had much of a choice. I wanted to evacuate my patient, but my superior—

I push the thought away as I place a far too aggressive checkmark on the clipboard I'm holding and then stomp out of the supply closet with a huff.

A pair of green-brown eyes connect with mine when I close—fine, *slam*—the door behind me. Dr Marina Moretti raises a delicate eyebrow. A gesture that shouldn't make my heart stutter against my sternum. Yet it does with this and many other things this woman does.

Maybe that's another reason I don't want to be here: the uncontrollable reactions and hormone spikes this woman causes in me. Or maybe she's the reason I haven't resigned yet and crawled back to Algiers. Not that I could admit that. What kind of self-respecting woman puts her career on hold for another person—who, as far as I can tell, isn't even interested in me *that way*.

'What did the door do to you?' Marina asks, her smooth voice slithering down my spine.

'Ah, the usual, you know? It looked at me the wrong way. Thought I would slam first, ask questions later.' I cringe at the words pouring out of my mouth. Being around this woman makes it harder for my brain to process things. Including, but not limited to, forming coherent sentences.

'Right…' Her voice trails off, but not before her lips twitch in a gesture I've learned to interpret as a smile. For how vibrant I've heard the Italians to be, Marina is far more buttoned-up than I expected. Though the more time I've spent near her, the easier it's been to understand her mannerisms.

'Anyway, how was your day off yesterday? Did Luca enjoy the petting zoo?' One of my patients the other day mentioned a temporary petting zoo setting up in a park not far from here. I had already forgotten this information until I bumped into Marina the day before yesterday. Though normally unreadable, the thundercloud around her was clear—or, well, *not* clear? That's how you identify a thundercloud, after all.

I'm still not sure what happened, but the need to lift her mood brought the memory back, and so I suggested she take the day off to decompress—thinking maybe she missed spending time with her son.

Now she sends me a smile broad enough to show me a glimpse of teeth. 'It was fantastic. Thanks for suggesting it. There was even a pony,' she says, voice more animated than it has been in days, and my stomach does a little loop.

'Oh, wow, did he get to ride it?'

Marina nods. 'Sure did. Do you want to see it?'

Her hand is already across the table to pick up her phone when I nod. Rounding the table, I stop right next to her and look down as she scrolls through the pictures of Luca feeding goats, cuddling a dog and then astride a pony with a huge grin on his face. 'Oh my God, he's so cute.'

Living with Marina also meant getting to know Luca, who is the embodiment of rambunctious—in the most flattering way. I wasn't sure what it would be like living with a child since I mostly prefer to be left alone, but I haven't met a person yet who wasn't charmed by this little boy. Within days, I found myself poking my head out of my room to see if he was around.

And yes, maybe in the process I would also get to see his mother. But that was *not* my intention.

'Now he wants to become a professional pony rider,' Marina says with a sideways glance towards me.

'Did you break the bad news to him that this isn't a real job?' I ask, laughing when she looks away.

'I'm not dashing the dreams and aspirations of a four-year-old,' she replies, expression severe except for the spark in her eyes that sends a wave of *something* down my body, making my knees wobble in a weird way.

Marina, thankfully oblivious to my body's rogue reactions, scrolls through a few more pictures before the screen changes and a phone call pops up from a number I instantly recognise.

'Coastguard?' I ask, and when Marina nods, I move to grab the emergency bags we have prepacked and ready to go at any time.

I toss the blue duffels—one for trauma, one for dehydration and basic wounds—onto the table. Marina grabs her keys and we're outside in less than a minute, my pulse knocking in my throat.

'The coastguard is escorting a small boat full of refugees ashore. They're reporting a woman in distress, some kind of abdominal bleeding, but they're not sure about anything beyond that,' Marina says, and in my head I'm already prepared for the worst as we speed off to the coordinates the coastguard gave us.

The air is heavy with that metallic-brine smell, the one that always clings to the island when the wind skims off the sea and brings with it all the scents of the southern Mediterranean. The drive to the port is less than five minutes, but I'm already building out my plan: hypothermia protocols, triage space, setting up a station for escalations. Even as my mind races, I'm hyper-aware of Marina beside me, knuckles whitening on the steering wheel as she takes the curves at double the limit with the blue lights of her car flashing.

At the port, the crowd is already gathering, a swarming, undulating mass of uniforms and volunteers and people with camera phones. The coastguard boat is nosing up to the concrete slip. A woman in a neon vest flags us down and yells something I barely register, but Marina is already out and running. I grab both bags and jog after her, willing my heart to calm. Each emergency can unfurl in different ways, and I like to be prepared for everything.

When we get to the dock, I can see the woman mentioned in the call lying prone on a stretcher with two people—her family?—kneeling beside her. My gaze sweeps over the rest of the assembled people, quickly categorising them and their needs. Most are already wrapped in their silver emergency blankets to ward off hypothermia, and no one seems to have any acute wounds. Shock more than anything else has everyone here rattled.

'Her first,' Marina says, arriving at the same conclusion.

When she charges forward, a man in a bulletproof vest and some kind of gun strapped to his front holds up a hand and says something. My step falters, eyes trained on his hideous weapon, but Marina is unperturbed. She shoots a slew of Italian back at him without stopping, and whatever she said has the coastguard member cowed enough to step back.

I follow Marina as she crouches beside the woman on the stretcher, gesturing at me to put the bags on the ground. Getting into a crouch next to her, I take in the scene: the woman's skin is waxy, her breaths shallow and ragged. Her lower abdomen is a mess of dried blood and sea-scummed slick, visible through the torn polyester of her dress. Her family—husband?—is hovering, his hands fluttering in front of him, eyes locked on Marina and me. He wants to be here; I can sense it. But the coastguard won't let him proceed until they have taken the details of everyone who has just arrived. Not that he could do much in this situation anyway.

She's in the best hands she can be, I try to tell him telepathically as our eyes lock. I'm not sure if it works, but his shoulders slump and he gives a resigned nod.

And I mean it. Though I may not have been here long, I've seen firsthand how much effort Marina puts into her clinic and into every person—refugee or otherwise—who comes through it for treatment. It's what I remind myself whenever I'm fed up with the situation I'm in: Marina has been an inspiration to watch, both as she works and when she's off duty. Though the second part might not be as appropriate as it should be.

Pushing away the heat that accompanies this thought, I focus on the woman in front of me. I unzip the bag, taking out two pairs of gloves and giving one to Marina before pulling my own on.

Marina's gloved hands are already hovering over the woman's abdomen as I hand her a pair of trauma shears. Without needing to speak, we fall into rhythm—cutting away the soaked, clinging fabric to find the source of the bleeding.

'I can't see where…' Marina's voice trails off when she moves the patient's shift. There's a fresh surge of dark blood. I swallow hard.

'Still active,' Marina mutters, more to herself than to me. She leans in, wiping clean gauze on the woman's lower belly, her focus narrowing on where the blood is coming from. When she moves lower, her eyes go wide. 'Could she be…?'

Marina doesn't get to finish her thought when I move to the woman's side and take her wrist gently, fingers searching for a pulse. 'Thready. Fast. She's crashing.'

Marina nods sharply. 'We need to get fluids in her now. You take the line—I'll manage the bleed.'

I grab a tourniquet and a sixteen-gauge cannula from the trauma bag. The woman's arm is a slim cord of tendon and sinew, veins ropy beneath salt-scorched skin. I pop the tourniquet and get the cannula in on the first go—thank God—but her blood wells sluggishly into the chamber. She's already on the edge.

'Bag's up,' I say, spiking and squeezing saline as Marina works the gauze deep into the crease between thigh and hip, fishing for the source.

'Can you give me some cover?' Marina asks, and I look up, scanning the dozen and more eyes on both of us. Then I look back down and see that even though her stomach is covered in blood, there is no wound.

'It's not external?' I ask as I move to the other bag, popping up a makeshift stand we keep at the bottom for situations like this when we require more privacy. Hanging the plastic sheet in a way so it drapes around us, I come back down and click on a penlight to give us more visibility.

'I think it's uterine. Maybe a ruptured ectopic, or—' I see her eyes jump, the maths clicking into place. 'Are you pregnant?' Marina asks, my heart jumping into my throat. 'The bleeding seems to come from your uterus, and if you are pregnant, the treatment could change.'

The woman opens her eyes, expression still pinched from pain, and she looks between us, uncomprehending.

'She doesn't speak English. Let me try something else.' I lean down, voice gentle but urgent. '*Vous êtes enceinte?*' The woman still looks between us, panic rising in her expression.

She only stares, lips parted, as if she's forgotten the whole concept of speech. I glance up at her husband, who's straining against the arms of a younger coastguard.

Marina's voice is low as she says, 'We risk hypovolemic shock if we move her and it's ectopic. But if we wait—'

'—she might bleed out on this dock,' I finish for her. We both know the choice. I meet the woman's gaze again and try one last time, '*Hal ant hamilu?*'

Are you pregnant?

Her eyes widen in recognition, and then she presses out some words too jumbled for me to understand. The common dialect of Arabic in Algeria is heavily influenced by French, making it harder to understand other dialects. Throughout med school, I made sure to learn Modern Standard Arabic, but I'm not as fluent as I used to be. They might have come from Sudan or maybe Syria if she can understand me.

Her chest rises rapidly, skin now slick with sweat. Her eyes dart all around, as if she's too scared to say anything. So I grab her hand, giving it a tight squeeze, and wrestle a reassuring smile from deep inside me.

'*Nahnu huna li-nu'īnaka, wa lan nu'ukhbira aḥadan bi-shay'in*,' I say slowly, pronouncing each syllable while trying to stay as quiet as possible.

She must have understood me, for she blinks twice and then gives an imperceptible nod. I look up to Marina, and from her expression, I know I don't have to repeat myself. But I still give her a nod and then say, 'We have to stabilise and transport her.'

Marina nods and, as if on cue, the sirens of the ambulance service approach us. 'Tell her I'm going to stem the bleeding as much as possible. It will be painful, but we're doing everything we can to save her—them.'

I relay the message in stilted words, and then we start prepping her for transport. She's already on a stretcher, which will make it easier.

In a tense choreography, I grab the trauma tape and a folded rescue blanket while Marina clamps her fingers on the bleed. There's little dignity in field medicine, but we try our best to preserve it for our patients. Marina cuts her soaked clothing off for better access, and I wedge the blanket under her hips to tilt the pelvis up, hoping to slow the internal haemorrhage. The first unit of saline is already empty. I swap it for the second, squeezing hard, and can practically feel her systolic pressure crawling up a single point with every drop.

The ambulance doors clang open, and two EMTs hustle towards us with a trolley. One of them, a young woman with a trainee badge half-torn from her uniform, looks so pale I'm worried she'll topple first. I lock eyes and bark, 'You, here—help me lift, one-two-three!' and together we get the woman onto the trolley.

The man tries to break through the barrier of coastguard people, but he is weak from the journey he has been on for weeks potentially. My heart goes out to him, but when it comes to triage, keeping families together isn't a priority right now. Our clinic is small, and anyone who is non-essential will only be in the way.

I almost jump into the ambulance with the woman—the only thing stopping me is Marina's hand on my shoulder, firm and warm in a way that freezes me mid-motion.

'You stay,' she says, not quite a command but not the sort of thing you refuse either. I try to protest but she cuts me off, voice low and tense. 'You need to look after the rest of the arrivals—see if anyone needs transportation. I'll take care of her.'

'What if you need my assistance?' I ask, and something in my voice sounds off. Like for some reason I need to hear that she does need me. This has nothing to do with whatever weird attachment I'm conjuring up in my brain.

'I'll be fine. Take care of the people here.'

She's right. The rest of the arrivals, still clustered on the pier, are a shifting, shivering mass of silver blankets, each set of eyes hollowed by fear and exhaustion. I'm the only one with extensive medical training here, and I can't leave them in the hands of the coastguard. What if there's another incident? Some undiagnosed acute illnesses waiting to pop up?

Splitting up is the smart choice. So I nod. 'All right.'

Marina shoves her car keys into my fist. 'I'll meet you at the clinic when you're done triaging here.' She's already striding after the trolley, and I watch her go—an angular, determined silhouette in the dim glow of the port lamps.

I still want to follow. Instead, I'm left with a set of keys, the taste of adrenaline fading from my tongue. There's still work to do, so I force my thoughts away from Marina and our unnamed patient to focus on other people who need me.

It's why I'm here, right? To prove my worth and be somewhere people need me—even if in my fantasy, things would have looked different.

CHAPTER THREE

Marina

THE REST OF the day goes by in a whirl of activity. I've done everything I can to save the woman—Fatima—and her child, which isn't as much as I *wanted* to do. But after stabilising her, I had no other choice but to order a transfer to a larger hospital where specialists would take care of any further treatment. The clinic is too small to deal with complex cases like Fatima's.

As I finish up for the day, I make a note to get in touch with the hospital tomorrow and ask for regular updates. There was at least one person on that boat who knew her, and if I can ease their mind I'll feel like I'm doing something. Even if it isn't much.

Dragging myself upstairs requires far more energy than I have after a day like this, but I put one foot in front of the other until the front door of the cosy flat greets me. Plus, I need to relieve the babysitter for the day. She's a local girl who looks after Luca whenever I need her to in the evenings—which, surprisingly, is less and less.

And the reason for that is sitting on the couch right now with a book in her hand and my sleeping child's head resting in her lap. She looks up when I step through the door, giving me a tentative smile. A picture so ordinary it shouldn't knock me sideways: her hand curved protectively over his temple, thumb stroking a small circle. One loose strand has slipped from her bun and rests against her cheek.

Something low in my chest pulls tight.

'Isabella was about to put him to bed when I came up, so I took over. But then he asked if he could stay up until you arrived and, well...' Layla looks down with a sheepish smile, shrugging one shoulder. 'We got comfy on the couch, but he must have been more tired than he let on.'

I smile at the picture, enjoying it more than I should. When Agron was still alive, we would divide our work in such a way that Luca was never alone or cared for by people who weren't his family. Of course, under current circumstances, I can't be picky, and Isabella has been great with him whenever I've needed her.

But Layla—I hadn't expected her to click with Luca the way she has. It seems a hidden talent of hers: sneaking past my defences when I'm certain I'm fortified against any intrusions.

When she first arrived, I expected her to be one more temporary fixture—another well-meaning humanitarian New Health Frontier seems to attract by the dozen who'd eventually ship back to a city clinic with a spicy anecdote about field work. But here she is, quietly, persistently carving out a place for herself in our little unit.

The first time she offered to look after Luca when I needed to head out for an emergency, I thought she was being polite. But afterwards she kept seeking out time with Luca. Now the three of us spending an evening together in the living room is almost a regular occurrence.

I could get used to it.

Except that would be foolish for more reasons than I can count, but two stand out front and centre: Layla is transient, and she's never pretended to be anything else. When she arrived here, she was clear that this assignment hadn't been her choice, and I respect her honesty in it. I know a thrill seeker won't enjoy the work I do here, despite its importance.

But even if she wasn't with one foot out the door already, there's a far more obvious barrier: she's my co-worker. Ethics aside, getting entangled with a co-worker hasn't ended well for me in the past.

I wouldn't even be here in Sicily running this clinic if I had never got involved with Francesca. And if I had never landed here, I wouldn't have met Agron and Luca, or become his mum. Strange how the most awful time of my life has led to the greatest gift.

And I'm about to lose it all if I don't find a solution.

'Do you want me to put him in his bed?' I ask, setting down my bag next to the door.

Layla looks down at Luca, ruffling his wispy blond hair, and my chest squeezes tightly when she shakes her head with a small smile. 'No, it's okay. Sit down and have a rest. You must be exhausted if you're getting here after me.'

Layla nods at the armchair, and after a second of hesitation, I plop down. The cushions swallow me almost instantly, and the tiredness sinks deeper into my bones. I blink several times, forcing myself to stay alert. If I close my eyes now, I'm going to be asleep within seconds.

From here I can see the soft hollow at the base of her throat where Luca's hair has left a pale crescent. My fatigue recedes just enough to make room for awareness. Unhelpful. Persistent.

'How is our patient?' Layla asks, drawing my attention. 'What's her name?'

'Fatima,' I say, and even saying her name makes her more real, the memory of her pinched face and the way she clutched at my hand searing through my exhaustion. 'I want to check in on her tomorrow. She's at Ospedale San Michele, in ICU, I imagine. We stabilised her enough to make it through the trip, but…' I leave the *but* hanging.

Layla nods. 'You did everything you could,' she says, and the words are simple enough, but there's a kind of insistence in them. Maybe she's trying to convince herself too.

I shrug, or try to, but my shoulders barely move. 'It's never enough. But thank you.'

When Layla smiles this time, it's a subdued one, reminding me of the early days when she had just arrived here—clearly against her wishes. I'm glad she's warmed up to me, or at least to Luca, to let her guard somewhat down. Enough for me to learn something had happened in her last placement without any of the details.

Strange how that has been something rolling around in my brain in the last few days even though I have a whole host of more pressing problems than what's going on in the life of my reluctant roommate-slash-co-worker.

My eyelids grow heavy when another wave of tiredness crashes through me. When I let them fall closed for a second, a comforting picture appears in front of me: Layla and Luca sitting on the couch just like they are right now, waiting for me to come home and join them.

It's the same picture the Albanian authorities want to see—as unfair as I find their requirements. What they are looking for exists. Not in any tangible way, but still… I could envision it as my eyes remain closed.

Layla kneels in front of me, one hand resting on my shoulder when I open my eyes again. Her knees brush against mine, warmth bleeding through fabric and sending a tingle through my limbs. I sit up with a start, only for her to offer me a placating smile. 'You fell asleep, so I put Luca to bed. Maybe you should do the same,' she says, and from the grogginess clinging to me, I must have fallen asleep. She's close enough that I can see the faint freckle at the edge of her bottom lip. Ridiculous, the things exhaustion notices.

I flick my wrist to look at my smartwatch, but I can't remember when I came up here, so the time is kind of meaningless.

'It's only been twenty minutes,' Layla says, seeing my confusion.

Fragments of pictures float through my mind, far too vivid to be dreams even though I know that's what they are. As if pretending hard enough would make it all fall into place on its own and solve my problem for me.

Pretend. The word gets stuck in my brain—just as the pictures have—and I look at Layla for far longer than is appropriate. She doesn't shy away from my intense stare, her dark brown eyes shimmering in the low light of the living room. She's become such a big part of Luca's life without either of us planning, and I can't even remember how it happened. She once looked after Luca when I had to attend an emergency and my usual babysitter fell through. And one evening was enough for the two to form a bond. A part of me knew back then it wasn't a good idea for me to let someone so temporary into Luca's life when he was just getting used to his father's death.

But then I thought he'd also lost enough already. If he finds some comfort—a new trusted adult outside of me—in her, how could I possibly take this away from him?

'Are you okay?' Layla asks, still not moving away—her hand *still* on my shoulder. The moment I become aware of it, the patch of skin beneath her touch starts to heat, and the burst of warmth trickles down my arm. I should move. I don't.

I'm so tired, so desperate for a solution, I almost tell her everything. But then I say, 'Yeah, I'm fine. Just a rough day with Fatima. Not often we get someone in such a critical state.' It's somewhat true. The fate of the patients I treat here is often grim when they escape war, famine and persecution in their home countries. Normally, my entire mind is focused on that and how I can mitigate the trauma they experience in their harrowing journey here. But with my own problems weighing me down, even the things I'm used to carrying feel heavier.

Layla's lips vanish into a thin line, and my eyes dart down to look at them for far longer than I should. 'You can talk to me, you know? In fact, I insist you do. From what I can tell, there isn't anyone else here to share the burden of everything,' she says, sitting back on her haunches and giving me an expectant look.

A thought rises in me as I look at her face, her expression so earnest. Maybe she could be the solution to my problem. I'm not about to find a real girlfriend in the time frame I need to secure Luca's adoption. But I don't need something real. No, just something *plausible* enough to withstand the scrutiny the agencies are going to put me through. For example, making sure I'm actually living in the same house as my wife.

No, I can't ask her that. It would be a breach of all the professional and personal boundaries we have in place. Sure, once the adoption is finalised, we would be free to go our separate ways—but technically Layla would be his other parent. It's an insane thing to ask of anyone, and I push it away as the impossibility it is. We don't know each other well enough for me to even indulge for a second in this thought.

Letting out a sigh, I sit up straight, and a gust of

chill sweeps through me when Layla's hand falls away from my shoulder. So I can't ask her to help, but that doesn't mean I can't talk about it, right? 'I'm not Luca's biological mother, but rather his adoptive mother—or at least hoping to be. When his father came into my life, Luca was six months old. Like you, Agron came here to work, and he brought Luca with him after fleeing a situation in his native Albania.'

I pause as the words come out haltingly; it's a story I'm still not used to telling. Really, the only person who knows everything is Giuseppe. 'And again, like he did with you, Luca grew on me from the moment I met him. It's a talent he's only honed as he's grown older. Living and working together and also sharing the occasional struggle, Agron and I became friends. Honestly, it happened so naturally, I don't remember when I realised I'd become Luca's other parent.'

Layla shifts her legs from under her, but even when I indicate the spot next to me, she stays seated on the floor with her back against the coffee table. Her eyes flicker away from my face, and I'm not sure why, until she asks, 'Were you and Agron…?'

The question floats between us, and it takes me a few seconds to catch up with it. My eyes go wide, and I shake my head—maybe a bit too vehemently for an inference that lots of other people would have reached. A man and a woman doing something like that is the default and, as much as it may annoy me, it doesn't make it less true. Or less aggravating.

But with Layla, I'm not shaking my head out of annoyance. It's more…she needs to know things aren't like that for me. Which is silly. Why would she need to know that?

'No, we were friends—best friends until he passed away. The way he talked about his wife, I don't think anyone could ever compete with her, even after her passing,' I say, remembering how fondly he'd spoken of Luca's mother. But then I hear what I have just said and add, 'Not that I *was* competing with her. Or trying to. I'm not into men.'

Great. That didn't sound weird or deflecting at all. And why do I even care? Appreciating Layla didn't equal any more than that, and I had good reasons for that. Reasons which had paid for this building and the starting capital I needed to become a part of New Health Frontier to operate as a free clinic.

If Layla thought any of my story weird, her face didn't let on. No, it stayed open and bright—almost too lovely to look at. 'I see, so Agron is the friend you said passed away last year. I'm sorry you had to deal with this on your own,' she says, and I push the distracting thoughts about her face away. Seems I've had to do it far too much these last few days. I really need to get a grip on things.

'Right, and...well, I think what you're seeing is the struggle of the adoption process taking a toll on me. Since Luca isn't an Italian citizen, it's not as straightforward. Because Agron passed away in a freak accident, he didn't have any contingencies like a will in place to make sure I was nominated as Luca's guardian. Ever since his death, the Albanian government has been content enough to let me take care of Luca. But now that they've received the official request for adoption, they're a bit more...reluctant.'

I should let it rest there. What do I have to gain from sharing more information with Layla? It's not like I'm not used to carrying burdens by myself, and there's nothing for her to do about it. But the talking is easing something inside my chest, which has remained tightly wound the last few weeks. Maybe I'm missing someone to talk to? I have Giuseppe, but whenever I talk to him, he is mainly concerned about the legal side of things.

Plus, if I do miraculously find a wife, I can't let him know how I happened upon this woman if it isn't legit. He'd be ethically bound to disclose things. When I told him I'm seeing someone, I could already see his suspicions rise. The less he knows about my thoughts the better.

'Oh, no, Marina. That sucks.' Layla frowned,

her genuine concern etched on her face. It was almost cute how much she cared about Luca. I say almost because I'm not supposed to find *anything* cute about a co-worker. 'What does reluctant mean? Like… You're his mother; that's clear to anyone who spends even a moment with him. Are they disputing that?'

I nod. 'They are. It has something to do with Albanian adoption law. At least that's what the lawyers are saying. Communication across different lawyers and agencies isn't straightforward. If it's not the language building a barrier, it's the culture.' I pause, letting out a sigh as the rest of the story comes tumbling out. 'From what I understand, Albanian legislation only permits an out-of-country adoption into a two-parent household and only after some rigorous checks. They're not willing to consider my application because I would be—*I am*—a single parent. So…they're asking me to surrender him to the authorities and have him returned to Albania.'

The last words sink between us like a stone, just the way I expected. There's no easy way to say it—no sanitised version I could give to Layla to make it sting less. The pain of the reality of things is my constant companion at this point, and I haven't given up yet. But the outlook is getting bleaker by the day. Sometimes I indulge wild fantasies of just grabbing him and leaving—finding a place where nobody knows us and where we can live in peace. But I wouldn't even know how to put this into action.

This idea is so far away from legal, I think Giuseppe would be calling the authorities if I let him know my thoughts. Layla, however, feels like a safe option. And by the way her face falls, I can tell she's dismayed to reach the same conclusion I reached during my call with Pepe earlier today.

'Wait, they want to take him back to Albania? Does he have any other family there that's waiting for him?'

My heart squeezes tight when Layla says *other* family, affirming the version of my life I know is true, no matter what the authorities have to say. I *am* Luca's family, have been his second parent for the last three and a half years of his life. It's the reminder I need to tell myself when things look hopeless.

I shake my head. 'None. He would enter into the foster care system in Albania, which is ridiculous. They have someone here willing to take him—not even relying on any government payments like childcare allowance I'd be entitled to. But because they have some rules that hark back to two centuries ago, they'd rather rip him from the only family he has than admit the rules are dumb and find a way around it.' I take a deep breath when I feel the panic from earlier this morning rising again. 'I won't let that happen, but my options are becoming more limited with each passing day.'

Layla's expression turns stricken, squeezing my chest even tighter. I don't know what I expected from her as the words bubble out, but it's clear she cares. Maybe enough to…?

'There has to be something we can do,' she says. 'You said you've spoken to lawyers. Is there anything I can do to help? Write letters of support? Character witness?'

Of course she'd want to help, but I shake my head again even before she's done speaking. 'Showing up with a wife and a genuine marriage certificate is the only way my lawyer thinks we can win the goodwill of the adoption authorities in Albania. They're not willing to budge otherwise.'

A line appears between Layla's brows, eyes drifting downwards as if contemplating. I can see the wheels turning in her head. 'And *any* spouse will do? It doesn't have to be a man?' she asks, her thoughts taking a similar route as mine did earlier.

'My lawyer consulted with some specialists in Albania, and the legislation doesn't specify the sex of the parents. It only names "two parents" as a requirement,' I say, though the details seem almost irrelevant because none of it would be real anyway. The time frame in which I need to deliver this marriage certificate is too short for any genuine romance. And I don't have the desire for anything real—or fake, if I'm being honest.

Layla nods, as if hoping this would be the answer. Her eyes flit back to me and when our gazes clash, there's a steel in hers that hits me square in the chest. Some weird premonition hits me where I somehow know what she's about to say, but even so I'm blindsided when she says, 'Okay, I'll do it then. Let's get married.'

CHAPTER FOUR

Layla

'ABSOLUTELY NOT.' I expected this answer from Marina, but it doesn't deter me. Quite the opposite—she's being stubborn for no good reason, and I'm determined to change her mind. There's something I can do to help her keep her family intact, and that is what I'll do.

Maybe this is the reason I was brought to this place—the reason I faced so many challenges at my old post to the point where I thought the politics and the backstabbing would break me. But what if it was some guiding hand placing these obstacles in my way so I would arrive here? To help a mother keep her child when cruel forces tried to separate them?

So, I ignore her refusal. 'How long does it take to get a marriage licence signed? I don't know anything about Italian bureaucracy, but I should have all relevant papers with me.' With how volatile some of the placements with New Health

Frontier can be, the organisation advises people not just to travel with their passports but also documents like birth certificates and other relevant things. I have all my stuff in a waterproof pouch at the bottom of my suitcase.

Marina shakes her head—something she's done far too much in the span of our short conversation. 'I can't accept that.'

'Why not?' I prompt when she doesn't elaborate because I genuinely don't understand. It's not like I'm attached to someone else, and since it doesn't matter that I'm a woman, it's the perfect solution. Even though the thought of fake marrying Marina kicks something loose at the bottom of my stomach.

I can't focus on that, or on the fact that she confirmed her interest in women through this conversation. With how liberal I wear my rainbow paraphernalia—from sneakers to lanyards to countless pins dotting the outside of my backpack—I'm sure she's picked up on the *subtle* clues about my preferences.

Wait, why am I even thinking about this? It's a fake proposal—preferences can't and won't factor into any of this.

When she doesn't say anything, I continue, 'I was lucky enough to grow up in a safe environment, but it doesn't mean I didn't see strife, too. My mum left her career, her family—all so I could have choices she didn't. If I can help Luca stay with his family, she would be furious with me if I didn't help.'

I look at Marina. 'And Luca—he doesn't get a say in any of this. He's just a kid who might grow up thinking he wasn't worth fighting for. I can't let that happen. Not when I can actually do something.'

Marina sighs, slumping forward and bracing her arms on her thighs. 'It's not appropriate for me to ask an employee to commit marriage fraud with me.'

I shrug, though the word 'fraud' stands out to me. She's right, of course. The marriage would be on paper only, but this wasn't to get some undue payout or anything like that. It's keeping her family intact. Under these circumstances, we'll surely find forgiveness from the powers in the universe.

There's no way anyone can stand by and let a boy be ripped away from the only family he's ever known. There's no way *I* can stand by and let it happen.

'But how are they going to know? We already live together, so that's a plus point. No need to fake things there.' As I say it, I know it cannot be this simplistic. But the difficulty of this task can't be what dissuades me from doing it. 'This is Luca we're talking about. I can't sit here and do nothing.'

Something in Marina's expression changes—softens in a way I rarely see in this resolute woman. But on the rare occasions I've seen her defences come down, the effect has been breathtaking. It is so now, too. My lungs squeeze all the air out of my body without letting any back in until I force my brain to override this baser instinct taking over whenever I look at Marina for too long.

That could be another complication in this plan, but I won't think about it now. It's not like Marina has shown any interest in me outside of the professional setting we live in.

'It involves a lot more than living together. Both the Italian and Albanian agencies will want to interview us, make sure we are a suitable couple and the best option for Luca,' Marina says, and there's a very clear undertone in her voice that sends a shiver down my spine. It's like she read my earlier thought and is repeating it back to me.

I may not have any interest in you, but this idea requires us to know things about each other. Well, the joke's on her; I *want* to know things about her, just as much as I *don't* want to know things. And the reason for it is the same—I'm not supposed to be here. So much that I'm actively talking to my contact at New Health Frontier to see how fast I can be transferred to a different place again. A field hospital, preferably set somewhere in a crisis zone.

But Marina—or maybe it is Luca's disarming charm that's actually to blame—makes it harder by the day to remember this is temporary. Even though the clinic is small and the workload swings up and down every day, I can see how much effort and passion she's put into establishing herself in a community that isn't always thrilled to know what she's doing.

There are enough people who view asylum seekers arriving as a nuisance instead of the desperate humans they are.

'Okay, so we'll set some time aside to quiz each other. We can start right now.' I take a deep breath. 'My name is Layla Sabri, only child of Samira and Muhammad, who still live in Algiers. I used to live there too until I joined New Health Frontier right after finishing up my medical training. From there, I—'

I stop when Marina raises her hands. 'This isn't the kind of thing I meant. It's more to sell the fantasy of a…couple. I've never mentioned a wife until this moment, so I'd expect them to be suspicious. Enough for their questions to be probing into places two *co-workers* definitely wouldn't know about each other.'

Again, Marina does most of her communicating through her tone rather than her words. It's a quality I've grown to admire about her. She possesses a subtlety when handling both our neighbours and the various patients coming into the clinic that puts me in awe every time I see her talk them down from something.

It's something I wish they taught at med school. Sure, they spend some time talking about bedside manner and all things related to that. But so much of working in medicine is much more than just the specific knowledge in the medical field. It's political manoeuvring, knowing when it's necessary to push and when things need to rest.

If I had the same skills in that regard as Marina has, I feel like maybe things at my last post wouldn't have ended the way they did. Maybe I would have somehow found the words to defend myself. But instead I got stuck with the blame for a bad call I didn't make.

I give her a slow nod, hopefully projecting that I understand the severity of this. Can she not tell my mind is already made up? 'I can't make you accept my help, but know that you can't talk me out of this. I'm not going to sit by if I have the means to help you keep your son here—dodgy or not.'

Marina slumps back, sinking further into the couch. I catch a glimpse of it again: her reluctance fading away. She lets out a deep sigh and before she can reject me again I say, 'What's the worst they can ask us? How we met? That's easy; just tell them we met through New Health Frontier. What else would they want to know? How often we sleep with each other? If you are more of a giver or a pillow princess?'

I don't regret the words *per se*, but when they come out of my mouth a burst of heat flares through me as unwanted pictures come alive in front of my mental eye of Marina decidedly *not* being a pillow princess. No, that would be me and only in those intrusive fantasies I can't get a grip on. None of which I've ever put into reality.

Oh crap, maybe she's right, and this is a terrible idea.

Her mouth twitching is the only sign of amusement I get from her before she turns serious again. 'Not in those exact words. But we'll have to prepare for anything, even if we might not be comfortable. Touching each other—holding hands or a kiss on the cheek—needs to feel natural. The same goes for talking about each other.'

Her chaste description of touching doesn't really help me maintain my distance from the absolutely un-chaste fantasies still flitting about my brain. I didn't give the idea of PDA any passing thought, but it's not like this is going to stop me. There're far greater things at stake here than my own comfort levels, and I won't be distracted—or dissuaded—by any of it.

'If you can do that, I can too,' I say with a bit more challenge in my voice than necessary. But I want to show her I'm not about to back down or flake on her.

'I'm prepared to do anything to keep Luca here with me, and some archaic legislation from two centuries ago isn't going to stand in my way. I'm just...concerned about the power dynamics here. I'm still working with you in a supervisory capacity, and you're living in the space I own. The last thing I want is to put you in an uncomfortable situation where you feel like you were pushed into things you didn't actually want.'

Marina leans back, exhaling slowly. When she speaks again, her tone has shifted—still firm, but less like a wall and more like a warning she doesn't want me to ignore.

'If we do this, we do it properly,' she says. 'There'll be paperwork between us—something that sets out what this arrangement is and isn't. We'll agree on what we tell the authorities, what happens after the adoption is finalised, and that you won't ever be held to any legal or financial obligations once it's done. A kind of...prenup, if you like.'

Her eyes meet mine, steady and clear. 'You'll have it in writing that I don't expect anything beyond the signature. You're not signing your life over, Layla. I want you protected as much as Luca.'

She makes a point of looking at me as she says it, and her concern touches something inside my chest—the place still bruised from my experience at my last posting. If my supervisor back then had cared even half as much about my comfort, maybe I would still be there and would have defended myself against the bad call they blamed me for. If I hadn't already been convinced to do this, Marina assuring me how aware she is of the power balance between us and pointing out the potential pitfalls would have been enough to put me at ease.

'At the end of the day, this has nothing to do with us and our working relationship,' I say with a smile I hope reads as unconcerned. 'This is about Luca and what's best for him. That's all I'm thinking about, and I know it's all you have on your mind as well.'

Marina nods, no hesitation in her action. 'It is. I didn't plan on asking this of you, but since you offered… I don't know if there are any other paths open.'

There's a pause, and the unspoken words make my heart bounce against my sternum. The very last *legal* path she sees open—and with how directly she used the word 'fraud', even that side of things is questionable. But Marina wants me to be aware of what I'm getting into, and I appreciate that.

I nod, my intention resolute. 'Let's do it, then. Tell me what I need to do.'

CHAPTER FIVE

Layla

THE COURTHOUSE SMELLS like lemon disinfectant, which tickles an ancient memory in my mind of my mother wiping all the counters down every morning before I went to school. Nothing suspicious about it as a kid, but now I wonder if her daily routine ever ground down on her the way it does to me when I stay rooted in place for too long. It's the reason—along with making a difference—why I signed up for New Health Frontier instead of choosing a more stable post as a family doctor in Algiers like my father wanted. But seeing my mother remain cooped up all her life planted an early seed inside me of yearning for a different life. One of freedom and travel and fun.

It's the same reason why marriage—relationships in general—never appealed to me. Tying myself down to someone just seems like a recipe for disaster when my ambitions and career could take me anywhere. I'm certainly not willing to compromise, and I wouldn't want anyone to do the same on my behalf. It's not that I've never been tempted. There were chances—flirtations during fieldwork, the occasional kiss that never went anywhere—but nothing I let root. It always felt safer to keep things fleeting. Safer not to owe anyone a piece of myself I couldn't take back.

So the irony isn't lost on me that I'm standing in this courthouse at the edge of town, waiting to tie myself to Marina Moretti.

A few days have passed since our initial conversation and nothing has changed about my resolve: I'm not going to let this little boy be deported to a country he doesn't know to live in an orphanage with other kids when he has a stable and loving home here.

And maybe my low opinion of marriage is the reason I feel so comfortable faking it. I never planned on getting married—or having kids—so looking at the other couples standing here in various states of dressed up is strange. The feeling crawls up my skin as I look around and try my best not to look like an imposter—whatever those look like.

Marina and I stand in the echoing atrium, clutching our folders, waiting to approach the service window. There's a sign taped to the counter, in four languages, that says: 'No Assistance Without Number'. So we hover, pretending that this whole thing—the two of us, about to convince both the Albanian and Italian governments that we are madly in love to the point where we tied the knot in record time—isn't the most ridiculous thing either of us has ever done.

Marina is in a skirt suit I've never seen her wear. I stopped dead in my tracks when she stepped out of her room, and it took me a few seconds to get my thoughts back in order. So used to seeing her in scrubs or casual wear, I was unprepared for the effect seeing her bare legs would have on me. Or how my mouth dried up when my eyes travelled down her body until I reached her feet. She'd swapped her usual Crocs for heels, which, duh—of course. But oh wow, I still wasn't prepared.

Am not prepared as I steal sideways glances at her. She keeps smoothing the front of it, even though there's not a wrinkle to be found. Every third breath, she tugs at her hair like she's considering yanking it out and running for the door. The nerves are contagious: I keep checking my watch, as if there's any reason to be anxious about being late to a marriage neither of us actually wants. I can't decide whether I should have dressed up more or if my plain navy trousers and white button-down are the more honest approach. Either way, we look like a pair of mismatched paper dolls, here to play house for some faceless bureaucracy.

'Number?' The voice is hard to hear at first, coming through an inch of glass and a speaker that has to be from the last century. Marina jumps and I almost drop my folder. I hand over our crumpled ticket: forty-four.

The clerk, a thin woman with reading glasses on a chain and a face like she's been personally wronged by every applicant, squints at our forms. She gestures for us to come closer, and we shuffle up to the window. There's a short exchange in Italian that goes right over my head and ends up with Marina directing me to drop the folder in a now-opened compartment under the window. When I do so, the clerk slams it shut and misses my fingers by millimetres. 'Purpose?' she asks in English, her Italian accent crisp and bored. Did Marina ask her to speak English in that last exchange?

I open my mouth, though nothing comes out. We've gone over the entire process, but now that I'm standing here, my mind goes completely blank and I just stare at the unamused clerk.

Marina, noticing my frozen state, says, '*Pubblicazioni di Matrimonio.* To be posted today.' She pauses, looking around and then bending closer to the glass, as if to avoid anyone listening in. 'I spoke to Salvatore Greco, and the Mayor assured me this would be handled right away.'

This is news to me, and I make the mistake of letting it show on my face. Marina knows the Mayor? And more, she spoke to him about us? She went over the legal requirements of the marriage, one being a *declaration of intent*—a document which needs to be published at least eight days before a wedding can take place. While going over all my documents, she said that she wasn't entirely sure if the declaration would be enough for the Albanian agency, so the moment the timer was up, we would still have to sign the actual marriage certificate. But since we were working on a tight deadline, she would see if she could pull some strings and get a waiver from the town hall.

And by town hall she'd apparently meant the flipping Mayor himself.

The clerk, with her supernatural ability to seemingly suss out weird turns in the process, looks up with one arched eyebrow. 'I'm afraid he's not in today to verify these claims,' she says, and I see Marina's shoulders tense. From our conversation in the car, she wasn't expecting it to be a hard process—just a drawn out one.

'*Tiziana, lo sai che non inventerei mai certe cose su Salvatore.*' I catch the irritation in Marina's voice, along with the clerk's name: Tiziana.

They volley a few more sentences in Italian. The only word I catch is *imbarazzante*, which I don't need a translation for. Tiziana glares at me like I'm guilty of marriage fraud *and* tax evasion to boot. I plaster my most innocent, regulation-compliant smile on my face and hope it makes me look less suspicious.

'You,' Tiziana finally says in English again, nodding at me. 'When did you become a resident of the commune?'

I blink. Right. Marina prepared me for the eventuality of questions and drilled me on my arrival dates, how and when I registered as a resident and all of that. I asked her if we needed some details about our *relationship* as well, but she waved it away. Apparently, all they are interested in today are dates and specifics about my status here. Though with the gleam in Tiziana's eyes, I'm not sure that's still true. By the way Marina shuffles next to me, hands swiping over her skirt in a nervous tic, I'm not sure she still believes it.

I certainly don't.

'A month and three weeks ago,' I say, down to the day.

Tiziana purses her lips, slaps a Post-it note on the folder containing all our forms and legal documents and writes something, then flips to another sheet. 'And the two of you—how long together?'

My gaze darts to Marina. We've practised this answer, but now I'm no longer sure it is enough. After going over my documents, we discarded the idea that we met when I first arrived, fell in love and decided we don't want to wait any longer. But rather, we met online—plausible enough in this day and age—and we began our relationship long distance before I got the opportunity to move here. This should signal some more stability, should anyone ask. Like Tiziana just has.

'Nine months,' I say, and out of the corner of my eye I see Marina's jaw tense, a millisecond of a wince that sends an arctic chill through my insides.

Tiziana circles something on the form. 'Very fast,' she says in a way that's less a comment and more a verdict. 'Who arranged the introduction?'

I freeze. We discussed meeting online. But online *where*? Tinder? Some online game? Maybe a doctor-specific forum and we just got chatting? In reality, I got dumped here by my NGO and wound up in her spare room. None of this spells *romance*, and yet I do have this particular buzz in the back of my neck whenever I look too long at Marina. Not that I do that. No, that would be weird.

'Special circumstances,' Marina says when I stay quiet, her voice steady and cool, but I can hear the crackle of nerves underneath. 'She was assigned to me as a remote worker first, to get her acclimatised to the clinic and the paperwork we do here while they sorted out her visa. We got chatting and hit it off.'

The last sentence comes out far more quietly than the words before, and my head whips around to look at her. Something about what she said hits me in a place low on my body, burrowing through my skin and into a squishy place.

We hit it off. It's an innocuous thing to say. People probably say that to each other all the time. It doesn't even have romantic connotations. Why am I reacting like it does?

The clerk sighs, stamps a piece of paper and slides a pair of forms through the tray at the bottom of the glass. 'Fill these,' she says. 'Then we have the interview.' She looks at me, eyebrows arched. 'You speak Italian, yes?'

I shake my head. She makes a note on the sheet in front of her, which I can only assume is labelled 'troublemakers'.

Marina leads us to one of the wooden benches lining the wall and I flop down beside her, already filling in the blanks with my best bureaucratic block letters. The form is simple: name, date of birth, address, previous marriages—none, none—and emergency contacts.

There's a pause. The only sounds are the squeak of my pen and someone yelling in the next room. Then Marina says, 'I think we need to accelerate this "getting to know each other" plan. We are one accidental revelation away from blowing this up.'

I nod, already on edge. 'What's our origin story, then? You already started with some details. So we met online as part of my training nine months ago and hit it off. Do we need more than that?' Something slips down my spine when I repeat her words, and I try to shake it off. 'I didn't know there would be an interview.'

Marina's expression turns dark. 'There normally isn't. I think Tiziana is being nosy as hell, but since it's in her power to deny us the declaration of intent, I wasn't about to kick up a stink. No doubt she's back there finding someone else who can sit at the counter so she can interview us personally.'

'This feels personal.' The words—and the insinuation—are out before I can consider what it means. Or if it's even appropriate to say.

Marina doesn't answer right away. Then she leans in, her voice pitched low enough that only I can hear. 'Tiziana and I went to high school together.' She says it as if she's reciting a diagnosis. 'We've been feuding since before the euro existed.'

I almost snort, except there's nothing funny

in the way she's glaring past my shoulder at the clerk's window. 'You mean like, actual feuding?'

Marina nods, lips pressed into a flat line. 'She was president of the student council. I was head of the biology club. There was an…*incident.*' She waves one hand as if swatting at a memory. 'It's not important. Point is, she is pathologically invested in making my life difficult.'

'Is the…incident going to come up in the interview?' I ask, pen hovering over the last box on my form. I can't tell if this feud is the kind of thing that leaves someone hiding under the cafeteria table or the kind that ends in egged cars and restraining orders. Knowing my luck, it's both.

Marina shakes her head. 'No. She'll try to poke holes in our story, but it's not like she's going to bring up the time I sabotaged her campaign posters with live mealworms.'

I nearly drop my pen at the admission. It forms a new picture of Marina in my head, one that has slightly rounder edges than the serious version I'm so used to. 'You didn't do that. Did you?'

She shrugs, eyes flickering with something dangerously close to pride. 'They were a metaphor. For the corruption in her campaign.'

I wheeze, trying to keep from laughing out loud, and the tension in my chest thaws just a little. 'Okay, so if she's going to be petty, we just have to be…not petty?'

'We have to be perfect,' Marina says, her voice suddenly brittle. I can tell she's not only worried about Tiziana, or the interview, or even the paperwork. She's worried about Luca, and about what will happen if this all comes crashing down. The weight of it is in her posture, her hands, the set of her jaw.

I want to say something reassuring, but I can't decide what would help, so instead I focus on the forms and the shaky script we cooked up the night before. We weren't anticipating being quizzed, so all the plans we made about 'getting to know each other' were for a point in the near future. Guess we're about to be tested on our ability to improvise.

I finish my form, double-check everything, and hand it to her. 'Should we hold hands for the interview?'

She blinks, then looks down at her own hands as if she's surprised to see them there. I've come on too strong, haven't I? It's not like there's a guide on how to treat the sort-of friend that you're about to marry to commit marriage fraud.

'I don't know,' she says, but she doesn't sound sure. 'Let's see how it goes. I imagine she'll be a problem no matter what we do.'

The door next to the bench opens and, as Marina correctly guessed, Tiziana calls us in, with a flat and bored-sounding, 'Next.' The interview room is smaller than I expected, filled with the same lemon-scented air and cheap government furniture. There's a round table, three chairs and a poster explaining, in cheerful pastels, the penalties for lying under oath.

Oh, great. Does this declaration of intent count as an oath? I should have thought of that before I came here. Well, here goes nothing.

We sit side by side. The clerk sits across from us, reading glasses now perched at the end of her nose. She opens a thick file, clicks a pen and starts. 'You said you've known each other for nine months. How long have you lived together?'

'Seven weeks,' I say, because at least that part is true.

Tiziana makes a noncommittal sound and flips to another page. 'Describe, please, how you decided to marry. Who proposed?'

The air in the room is suddenly sharp enough to slice bread with. I scramble for a believable answer, but Marina launches in with her clinical voice. 'We discussed it,' she says, 'and determined that formalising our relationship would provide stability for…our son.' Her words are perfect, but her hands have twisted together so tightly her knuckles go white.

'Your son?' Tiziana repeats, pen poised.

'Luca,' I say, and give the most natural smile I can muster. 'He's four. Neither of us are his biological mother, but he's been in Marina's care for…for years now. I joined them some weeks ago after we decided it's the right time. We want to provide a stable home for him.'

Something in the clerk's expression softens as her eyes dart between us before writing down something else. 'Ah, so even though your relationship is still new, you decided on this step because it's in the best interest of your child. They are so precious,' she says, and I swallow a sigh of relief. So anything child-related will get us on her good side.

Marina nods, seemingly reading my thoughts. 'With the age he's at, we're also actively thinking about his best interests when it comes to expanding the family. Us getting married is an important step for that.'

She reaches over and wraps her hand around mine, which is tightly wound around the shoulder strap of my handbag. A zap travels up my arm from where her fingers graze over my skin, and the touch is enough to replace the incredulous look on my face with a befuddled one. I'm not sure that's much better considering I should be used to Marina's touch. But it's better than Tiziana potentially thinking I don't want to have more children.

I don't even want to have the first… I think. I have to admit that being around Luca has been so different from how I imagined living with a child. But I'm far from responsible for him.

I try to be present, to manufacture a smile and make it sit there on my face like a store mannequin. The clerk continues, a metronome of doubts flicking her gaze from our entwined hands to the forms and back again. 'Signorina Sabri, what do you most admire about your fiancée?'

My brain hitches, throwing up a grey screen of static. I have a few well-rehearsed answers for job interviews and 'tell me about yourself' ice-breakers, but no one's ever asked what I admire about a person I'm supposed to be in love with. Especially not a person who just this morning had to talk me out of chucking a box of poorly categorised medical supplies out of the window.

'She cares,' I say, the truth coming out before I can even consider whether I should say it or rather stick with something generic. 'About people, helping them. A doctor of her calibre could work anywhere, yet she chose to dedicate her professional career to vulnerable people often villainised in society.' Regardless of how I feel about being here, the passion and sacrifice Marina has put into building the clinic is something I admire about her. Knowing what I now know about how she's come into caring for Luca only solidifies this opinion.

I pause when her grip around my hand tightens ever so slightly. How should I interpret the gesture? Does she want me to continue or shut my mouth? Probably the latter, but the way Tiziana looks at me compels me to go on. 'And not just that, she's a devoted mother on top of being an excellent and compassionate doctor. It's a hard balance to strike with the guilt people put on working mothers. I've seen it with my own mother, how she forewent a career she dreamed of to raise me. I know she loves me, but there is an air of regret around her whenever she talks about shutting down her tailor's shop. Getting wrapped up in motherhood alone without purpose outside of it is not healthy.'

Oops. That's way too personal. And judging by the fleeting expression in Marina's eyes before the usual impenetrable wall comes up, she doesn't want me going around sharing information about myself. Or talking about her as if I fancy her. Which of course I don't. Can you imagine the cliché? Liking the woman I've lived with for seven weeks and who I'm about to fake marry to make sure she doesn't lose her son to a faceless government entity?

Yeah, that's not my life.

Tiziana smiles a little, and it's so brief and so unexpected it makes me lose my train of thought. I start to twist my hand out of hers, but Marina holds it, squeezing just enough to keep me in place. As if she doesn't want me to let go. That can't be right.

'Layla's right,' she says, her accent getting stronger as she talks, which is the first sign I catch that she's nervous. Or maybe emotional? 'Neither of us had a stable childhood. My parents had…problems. So did hers. But each of us, on our own, decided that it stops with us and Luca. That's why we're doing all of this.'

I can't help but stare at her. Mostly because this is more personal than I've ever heard Marina get, but partly because she's still not looking at me. She's talking to Tiziana, but her words are for me, too. I feel it in my chest, all warm and fizzy, and for a second the rest of the courthouse—the lemon cleaning product, the flickering fluorescent light, even the battleaxe of a clerk—fades away and it's just us.

'So you see,' Marina continues, 'we may not do this the traditional way, but we are determined to give Luca stability. We want him to know he's loved. That he belongs.'

I swallow, because that is the rawest thing I've ever heard her say, and it's a side of her I've never experienced. My reaction to it is more instinctive than anything else—I flip my hand around, threading my fingers between hers. So much for the 'we don't need to hold hands' guidance.

But even as a warm shudder runs through me, I tell myself it's what people in love would do. It doesn't mean more than that, and I'd better not get carried away by stray hormones. With Luca involved, there's too much on the line here.

Tiziana scribbles a final note, snaps the folder shut with a sharp *thwap*, and fixes us both with a stare that hangs on Marina for a few seconds too long before flicking over to me. There's zero smile, not even a hint, but something shifts in the room. Have we convinced her?

I hold my breath, and Marina's fingers tighten around mine once more.

'We'll publish your declaration today,' Tiziana says, all business and no hint of her initial hesitation. 'To sign the marriage certificate, you must call and make a new appointment for you and your witnesses, with the first day of the declaration's expiry being the earliest appointment possible. Understood?'

I nod, a little stunned, while Marina's grip on my hand loosens just enough that I can actually breathe again. There's a shuffle as Tiziana prints out a receipt and slides it across the table for us to sign.

'Is there anything else?' Marina asks. Her voice is stiff, almost too polite, but I can tell by the way her eyes flick over to me that she's still wound tight. I know we convinced the clerk, and we have to take this win as she's the first of many who will scrutinise us.

And there's no doubt in my mind about what we're doing. Luca is counting on us.

Tiziana shakes her head with a little upward jerk and says, 'That is all,' as she hands us the declaration of intent along with the folder with our documents in it.

We stand, both at once, and for a second, I think maybe we're supposed to hug or high-five or do something physical to prove we're a real couple. But instead, Marina's arm just hangs at her side, the knuckles gone white again. 'Let's go. I have to file the declaration with the lawyer so he can send it to the agencies to get things started,' she says when the clerk is out of earshot, and Marina is halfway down the corridor when my brain catches up with what she said and I hastily follow her.

Right, this was one of many boxes we need to tick. But we did it. We played a convincing couple. All that's left for me to do is get a grip on the sparks of attraction appearing whenever we touch. Because I know we will touch *a lot* and none of it can or will lead to anything because it's all performative.

Plus, my banishment to Sicily is temporary until things have blown over, and then New

Health Frontier will redeploy me. I just have to continue to ask them. But I know I will wear them down. My future is not here.

CHAPTER SIX

Marina

'DO YOU LIKE CHOCOLATE?' It's an innocuous question and I can't imagine it will ever be relevant again, but I go with it anyway. It's something I should know about my spouse, right? What if one of the social workers asks me about her preferences and I tell her she likes dark chocolate, only to learn during the interview she's allergic to it?

They wouldn't hesitate to deny my adoption of Luca even though I've so far jumped through all the hoops they've held in front of me.

My eyes drift towards Luca, who is standing with a group of children at a small table. Every pair of tiny hands is smeared with chocolate as they sample every flavour imaginable the shop has to offer. Three employees of the chocolate store supervise the children, giving them a description of each sample as if they were dealing with the most refined palates.

The entire experience is extra, and I'm here for

it. I can't even remember the last time I left Pozzallo to do something fun. My life is so wrapped up in the adoption battle and the clinic, I've forgotten what it's like to leave my shell and live a little. That's until Layla barrelled into my life, upending it in ways I couldn't have imagined.

She's standing next to me, phone held up as she takes a picture of the chaotic scene in front of us as the kids eat enough chocolate to put the entire room in a diabetic coma. It was Layla's idea to come here to ChocoLù, which offers tasting tours for kids on the weekend. It was after I suggested we should sit down and hammer out the details not just of how we met but what we know about each other.

Being grilled by Tiziana showed me just how little I've thought about this entire scheme and she caught us unprepared. I'm honestly not sure if I would have made it out of the interview without Layla and her quick thinking around the questions.

She cares.

Her words keep popping into my head unbidden and, no matter how often I swat at them, they keep circling back like the fragment of a melody when you try to recall the entire song but all you can catch are wisps of notes. This is what happens when I think back to that moment—or even just look at her. She reminds me of something. A very particular something I thought I'd left behind in Milan for good.

'I do,' she says with a wide smile. 'When I was little, every Eid we'd get those chocolate coins in gold foil. My cousin didn't like chocolate, so I'd trade her my coins for these weird marzipan animals she got instead. I thought I was doing her this massive favour—like a child saint making a noble sacrifice. Turns out she just wanted the shiny wrappers to decorate her doll's house. I was emotionally manipulated by a six-year-old with a glue stick and crafting ambitions for her doll's house.' She lifts an eyebrow at me. 'What about you? What chocolate did you have growing up?'

'Not really a sweets type of person myself,' I say when her expectant gaze lands on me, and the faux shock in her gasp makes me chuckle.

'I can't believe I'm about to marry a chocolate hater. That's actually a deal breaker for me, if I'm being honest.' Jokes like that have become more common between us—mainly from Layla. She has an easygoing nature I'm growing to admire more and more.

'Not a hater,' I correct. 'I just prefer savoury. If they served anchovies at birthday parties instead of cake, I'd have been the happiest kid.'

Layla narrows her eyes as if reappraising me, and I can read the mischief in her lopsided grin. 'I'm going to test that. Next time we go somewhere, you have to pick, but it has to involve something you consider a treat.'

The idea of a next time hits me square in the chest, heavier than I want to admit. She says it so casually, like she wants there to be more outings. Of course she does, because after what Tiziana put us through with the impromptu interview, Layla wants to be prepared. I want to be prepared too, though I'm questioning the wisdom of the chocolate shop setup as a venue for getting to know each other.

I know it's necessary, but I still can't shake the feeling I'm walking head-first into something I'm not ready for. And I don't mean the adoption or anything Luca related. No, that part is so easy. Becoming his mother has been like finding a missing piece I didn't know was floating around in the universe.

No, the root of all my concerns stands next to me, her scent so known to me yet still novel that I can smell it over the sugar and chocolate filling the room. It's not something I should notice.

I shouldn't be thinking about any of that, let alone cataloguing it. She's not just my not-wife, she's my subordinate and my houseguest. The last thing I need is to start associating that scent—something floral layered atop some spicy edge—with anything other than 'colleague' or 'helpful friend'. It's like my body didn't get the last memo, because half my limbic system is just a slideshow of every time she's ever laughed, or rolled her eyes, or stood close enough that the heat from her skin makes my heart rate jump by triple digits.

As she leans over to show me the picture she took, I claw back the memory of my time in Milan and what happened there. How I got entangled with my superior and when I broke things off with her, she dragged my name through the mud in front of everyone at our hospital. The investigations and accusations revealed her to be at the core of all the problems, and the hospital—initially taking her side—were scared enough to offer me enough funds to start my new life on Sicily.

And a lifelong lesson: don't ever get involved with a co-worker.

The photo she snapped is a small masterpiece of chaos: Luca's head is thrown back in laughter, cheeks streaked with cocoa, and his tongue sticks out, stained blue from some lurid concoction that was probably never meant for human consumption. He looks incandescently happy. Next to him are two other kids, faces streaked with sugar, all howling with the kind of bliss only small children or escaped zoo animals can muster.

'He looks so much like Agron here,' I say before I can stop myself, and I have to swallow hard against it.

Layla's smile softens. 'You miss him.'

I nod, waiting for the embarrassment to wash over me. It must look strange how attached I grew to this man who crashed into my life with his kid. Especially since Layla knows we were never more than friends—given I was quite explicit about my preferences. I know people have talked about what a strange pair Agron and I made and wondered how such a connection could even work. But I'm not picking any of this up from Layla. Her eyes have a curious and sympathetic spark in them. Like she somehow understands what he meant to me without me having to say anything.

And it's because of this openness that I say something.

'He never told me what brought him to Sicily. I suspect after losing Luca's mother, he needed to be anywhere else. But he didn't speak about his grief, only that he was alone with his son and looking for a better life. It's not an uncommon story for people arriving on my doorstep. People join New Health Frontier for a specific reason, and I'm just happy to give them a bed and training before they're off to some new adventure,' I say, and I don't miss the slight wince contorting her face.

But she catches herself as she nods. 'And then he decided to stay? I'm so curious about him, but please don't feel compelled to answer any questions.'

My stomach flips over as she says that—something about knowing she's curious about *me* sending a flutter through me that's entirely inappropriate. She's not asking because she wants to know things about me, I remind myself. No, things about Agron—the father of *my* child—are something I would share with my spouse. She's asking because that's why we're here: to exchange enough information to convince the people around us we are truly in love and ready to spend the rest of our lives together.

'I don't think he ever had a plan for what came next. His only concern was to find a place to settle down for the time being. Plus, I don't have a term limit or anything at the clinic. People can stay and work with me for as long as they like—given the funding is there, of course.' I look over to where Luca is talking to another child while waving a piece of chocolate in front of him. 'And when I grew closer to Luca, everything between the three of us just clicked. We became a family as time went on. When Luca one day called me "Mamma" it was a seismic shock to my life. I thought maybe I had crossed a line, pretending I'm something to him I'm not. But Agron just laughed, picking up Luca and asking him if he wanted me to be his mother and if I wanted to be his.'

I trail off as the memory flashes through my mind, clear enough to bring with it all the pain of his passing. It'll never go away, but I hope some day fondness will grow over it all. An appreciation that things had to happen this way for me to find my son—my family.

Layla looks at me, and it's suddenly far too much to handle here in a room saturated with melting sugar and shrieking children. I glance away, fuss over my coffee, but her gaze stays fixed—softly insistent. 'Thank you for telling me,' she says. 'I know he must've been special if he raised such an amazing kid.' Her smile is unguarded, stretched wide with sincerity. No pity, just a kind of awe that startles me.

I shrug, attempting nonchalance, but my throat is tight. 'He was a mess, but a good man. He would have liked you.' I regret it as soon as I say it, sure I've made things awkward.

But Layla only laughs and says, 'I would've liked him too. Anyone who can so selflessly build a new family is someone I would like to know.'

At that moment, Luca appears at my elbow, face gleaming with sticky triumph. 'Mamma, can I have the one with the chilli? They said it's for grown-ups, but Massimo got one.' His lips are already stained red from some raspberry monstrosity, but he looks so expectant I can't say no. Even though I know tonight will be full of wide eyes and bouncing off the walls.

'If you finish your water first,' I say, already knowing it's a lost cause: he'll be hyper until dawn, and I'll have to peel this little goblin off the walls.

Luca's already gnawing on the corner of the chocolate square before I finish the sentence, and he makes a face so comically stricken that even Layla snorts. 'No…' he gasps, tongue lolling, which earns him a cup of water from the nearest staff member and a round of applause from the other kids.

I watch him for a moment, more relieved than I should be that he's happy, that he's here and alive and mine for now, at least. The sugar buzz begins to hit him in real time—his eyes go glassy and he's hopping on the spot, conducting an invisible orchestra. For the moment, everything else—the paperwork, the looming interviews, the certainty that neither the Italian nor the Albanian government will be satisfied until they've wrung every ounce of sincerity from this sham of a marriage—recedes.

Layla watches him too, her chin in her hand, a small smile tucked away at the corner of her mouth. I should say something, but her presence is simultaneously comforting and dangerous. Like an old quilt left near a bonfire. I have no idea how to keep her at a proper distance.

Across the shop, a bell chimes and a woman in a pink apron claps her hands to get the parents' attention. 'The tour is finished!' she calls, and the sugar-high mob of children stampedes towards the exit, Luca at the centre.

I realise, as I'm collecting Luca's jacket from the floor and untangling him from an epic chain-hug of two other kids, that we've spent the entire afternoon talking about me. My life, my mistakes, my makeshift family. Or at least the bits I allow myself to share to make it believable. Layla has nodded, asked questions, offered up the occasional self-deprecating anecdote, but I don't know any of her real stories. How did she end up here, a thousand kilometres from anyone she's ever known? What did she lose along the way, or run from, or hope to find?

The notion sticks in my brain. I need to know these things if I'm going to pass for her wife. I should probably know more than that she has an alarming willingness to eat sugar for breakfast or how the lattes she drinks are an offence to any well-raised Italian.

'Why don't we go to dinner before we head back home?' I say as I wave to the last parent to leave and we step into the bright street, a slow-motion tide of sunset and the semi-feral children weaving between the tables at the café next door. Luca takes off at once, leap-frogging his way up the steps to a little piazza, where the other kids immediately pull him into a game of football with a half-deflated plastic ball.

Layla's eyes go soft at the invitation, like I've passed some secret test. She tucks her phone into her back pocket and says, lightly as can be, 'Is this our first official date, then?' She doesn't mean it, but the words catch in the air between us. I can't tell if the heat rising to my cheeks is from embarrassment or something else, but I have to clear my throat before answering.

'Let's call it a…strategic briefing over pizza.'

'A classic Sicilian romance,' she deadpans. 'You know I've never actually had proper pizza here?'

'How is that possible? You've lived here for nearly two months!'

She shrugs, hands in her jacket pockets. 'You cook at home most nights, and you're kind enough to feed me along with yourself and Luca. And the rest of the time… I don't know…it didn't feel right to go eat nice food by myself. Growing up, we only ordered pizza on the good days, after something big, like the end of exams or someone getting a gold star at school. It always felt like a reward, not something you just…do.'

The way she says it, offhand but with this

glossed-over gravity, makes me pause. I've imagined so many things about Layla with her bright smile and her outspoken personality. Her home life being restrictive has never entered my mind.

Was she escaping a life she wanted to shake? I want to know, though I doubt such a question would ever come up with the authorities. It's more about birthdays, allergies, where she went to school…

'Let me be the first one to introduce you to this way of life, then,' I say, the smile appearing on my lips feeling much lighter than things have been in a while. We're far from done, but something about this moment feels relaxed—almost effortless. 'We spent all day talking about me, but there's so much I don't know about you.'

Something intangible flickers over her expression, too fast for me to catch it, before the smile I'm used to from her drops back into place. 'Lucky for you, there's not that much to catch up. Until I left home last year, my childhood and medical school appearance was pretty straightforward. But yes… Let's have dinner.'

She pauses, her gaze drifting over the piazza, and an astonished laugh escapes my throat when she brings her fingers to her mouth and whistles. Luca's head snaps up not even a second later, and he looks around at his newly made friends before giving them a short wave and running towards us. He collides with Layla's leg, and she puts her hand on his head and gives his mop of blond hair an affectionate tousle.

I blink several times, grappling with my surprise. Partly at how easily he came running towards her—as if none of this is fake for him. Which is strange because we've decided not to tell him about any of the mechanics involved in his adoption.

But more than that—

'Did you whistle for him to come here?'

Layla looks at me, big eyes wide in a proclamation of innocence, but I see the sheepish smile she's trying to hide. 'I was teaching him how to whistle the other day.'

I clamp down on the laugh bubbling up in my throat. 'And while teaching him, you also trained him to come when you do whistle? Like a dog?'

As if waiting for his cue, Luca lets out a short bark, and it's enough to undo my serious facade and my laugh rings across the piazza just as the sun vanishes behind the buildings.

'It does seem rather straightforward,' I say, and I don't miss Layla's 'I told you so' face. It's strange that I even know she has a face like that. It's not an expression she would ever use with a patient, and yet I have a clear mental catalogue of Layla's faces and what they mean.

‘Do you want me to take over?’ she asks when I shift in my seat.

Luca smashed two pieces of pizza in his face, which must have set off some chemical reaction in a body mostly comprised of chocolate at this point. Because not even two minutes later, his head came down on the table as all the energy left his body.

Now he’s on my lap, face buried in my neck and his little chest rising in slow breaths. I shake my head. ‘No, it’s fine. He is still at the stage where he’s not too heavy.’

‘Are you speaking from experience? Younger siblings? Nieces and nephews?’ Layla leans forward, chin resting in her hand, and the light of the candle casts a glow over her tawny skin, making it almost shine from within.

‘Mostly theoretical knowledge from having studied humans for a long time. I have a sister, but she lives in Australia and—’ I interrupt myself when I notice what she’s doing. ‘You’re asking me questions again.’

Layla chuckles, and the sound slips over my skin and down my spine, settling in a place I don’t dare to look at too closely. ‘I thought the point was to get to know each other,’ she says. ‘I have to ask questions.’

‘And the point of dinner was that I finally get to know some stuff about you. But somehow you manage to turn things around and ask more questions about me.' The pattern of conversation unfolds in front of me as I examine it closer. 'Do you not like to talk about yourself?'

Layla laughs again, though this time it's more brittle. 'Do people ever like talking about themselves? Outside of narcissists, of course. I think they are absolutely delighted at the prospect.'

But there's an edge to her reluctance, a kind of practised evasiveness that goes deeper than garden-variety humility. I know the signs; I've spent years in exam rooms and waiting areas, coaxing stories from people who'd rather not. Most of the time I'm content to let things be, but with Layla, I want to know. Maybe because I have to. Maybe because under the circumstances I'm allowed.

So I take a stab in the dark. 'Or maybe you don't mind talking about yourself. Just not with me.'

Layla's eyebrows flicker upward, the accusation landing heavier than I intended. She looks away, feigning absorption in the flame of the flickering candle. I regret the words, but I don't retract them.

'I mean,' I continue, softer, 'outside of the narcissists. Some people have trouble talking about themselves because they've learned it's not safe.'

I have no idea if this is true—if her reluctance has something to do with her past or with me. But maybe guessing one way will show me whether I'm right.

She's about to answer when a crash rattles the plates behind the espresso bar, followed by a sharp, guttural shout. Chairs scrape across the tiles as a commotion breaks out two tables over. A heavyset man in a tank top lurches to his feet, swaying as he tries to keep himself upright. His wife, I assume, squeals and reaches for him, but he's already crumpling forward, eyes wide and unseeing.

My body moves before my mind does—a reflex burned in from too many nights on-call. I get off my chair, gently placing Luca on one of the sitting benches along the wall. When I get to the unconscious man, Layla is right there with me.

He's breathing, but it's shallow. The blue tint of his lips is unmistakable, even under the jaundiced lighting. His hand spasms, knocking over a glass. I look up—Layla's already at the carotid.

'Sir, can you hear me?' I say in Italian, loudly. No response. I reach for his wrist: thready pulse, barely there. He's diaphoretic, beads of sweat popping out on his brow. I snap my fingers in front of his face, but his gaze is fixed and sliding out of focus.

'Layla—' I say, not even finishing as we fall into the rhythm familiar from emergencies back in our clinic. She's already sliding her thumb in the man's mouth, checking for a blockage, then tips his head in case a seizure is coming. There isn't one, but his breathing is getting thinner and more ragged, and the thump of panic at my temples drowns out the tinny pop of the restaurant's sound system as the rest of the tables begin to notice.

'He's about to code,' Layla says in English, voice barely above a whisper. But I catch it. I always catch her voice, even in chaos.

'*Chiami un'ambulanza!*' I bark towards the staff.

Layla's adjusting her jacket on the floor to cover the remnants of food and glass, checking the man's airway, clearing his tongue from the roof of his mouth. I shift, wedge my fist into his epigastrium and try to roll him into recovery position, but he's a deadweight. He sags; his pulse flutters under my hand for a second, then dissipates like steam.

'Go time,' Layla says, reading what happened from my expression alone, and she's right. I exhale, plant my knees and start compressions. My hands are sticky with something—beer, sweat, some pizza remnants from helping Luca? Doesn't matter. I count out loud in English because it's the only way I know how to keep the rhythm. 'One, two, three, four...'

Layla listens at his mouth, shakes her head

and slaps him twice on the chest. She's muttering under her breath, a string of colourful French invectives I can't understand but instinctively approve of. Our audience is a growing half-circle of horrified diners. The clock above the bar tells me nothing useful except that there are seconds passing and not enough of them.

Finally, a pair of paramedics cut through the crowd, one carrying a battered orange kit and the other dragging a trolley. I can see immediately they're used to car accidents, not restaurant-side cardiac arrests. Their eyes go wide as I rattle off a rapid assessment—unconscious, no response to pain, pulse gone, airway clear, probable myocardial infarct or cardiac arrhythmia. We barely pause in compressions as the defibrillator is unpacked and leads slap onto the man's chest.

The monitor crackles to life, sticky pads clinging to sweat-slick skin, and one of the paramedics goes through the familiar information displayed on the screen. I don't need to look. I know the rhythm by now. Seen it enough times to recognise the twitchy, disorganised trace of a heart still trying to beat itself into order.

'Shockable,' Layla confirms, already nodding before they can finish. 'Charge to two hundred.'

She reaches for the paddles and for a second I think the paramedics might protest, but then they take one look at her face and defer with a silent step back.

'Clear,' Layla says, her voice sharp and pitched for obedience. Everyone steps back, and the machine delivers a jolt that kicks the man's torso clean off the tiles.

He slumps. Nothing.

'Still no pulse,' I say, pressing back to his carotid. 'Resuming compressions.'

I fall into rhythm again, ignoring the sweat pooling at the base of my spine. Layla takes the BVM mask from the paramedics and begins ventilating, syncing to my count without needing the words. She presses a hand briefly to my shoulder as I reach thirty, a silent exchange, and takes over compressions with a practised ease that leaves me able to reposition his airway and check for movement.

And then—

'Wait.' I pause, hand braced to listen again. 'There.'

It's faint. A shift under my fingers. A flutter that isn't mine.

'I think we've got something,' I say, and Layla's already repositioning the monitor. We all hold our breath as the jagged line on the screen starts to steady—irregular spikes at first, then a slightly more coherent rhythm. It's not normal—far from it—but it's there. 'Still thready,' I murmur, fingers on his carotid. 'But definitely there.'

'Respiratory effort's back,' Layla confirms, tilting his head and listening at his mouth. 'Shallow, but spontaneous.'

The paramedics shift behind us, but I hold up a hand without looking. 'Not yet.' We're not carting off someone in V-tach just because he's breathing now.

Layla nods at my unspoken thought. 'Check pupils?' she says, already moving to expose his arm. I get my pen torch and flick it across both eyes. Slow reaction, but present.

'Responsive to light. Still hypotensive though.' I glance at the man's face—ashen, waxy, but no longer grey-blue. A bead of sweat forms near his temple. A good sign. Circulation's coming back online.

She's got the cuff on his arm and is manually checking BP. 'Seventy over forty. Low, but we can work with that. Let's get IV access before he gets bundled off.'

The taller paramedic steps in, holding out a cannula, and Layla accepts it without pause, sliding it into the patient's forearm with the kind of efficiency that makes even seasoned emergency techs step back.

'Push fluids,' she tells them. 'One line open, monitor vitals continuously. Oxygen stays on.'

I finish taping down the IV line and double-check the ECG one last time. Still ugly, but stable enough for transfer.

I meet Layla's eyes. 'Okay?'

She nods. 'Okay.'

I turn to the paramedics, finally stepping back. 'You can move him now.'

They jump into motion, straps clicking, movements smoother now that the leadership baton's been passed back to them. The younger paramedic whistles low, eyes flicking to the monitor. 'Good job,' he says in Italian.

I'm too tired to reply, but Layla offers a tight smile as she watches them wheel him away. Some glass shards glitter on her trousers from where she's knelt, and her shirt is still soaked with whatever got spilled during the initial collapse. There's sauce on my forearm. Somehow, we both look like we've just come out of a war zone and not a charming seaside pizzeria.

'You okay?' I murmur once the trolley disappears through the back exit and the restaurant begins its slow, stunned return to normality.

Layla doesn't answer right away. She looks over to where Luca is still curled on the bench, undisturbed by the chaos.

'Yeah,' she finally says, brushing a damp curl from her temple. 'You?'

I consider lying. But instead, I just nod and let

the adrenaline bleed from my limbs. The waiter—shell-shocked but steady—offers us both glasses of water. I take one, nod my thanks and raise it to Layla like a toast.

'To not letting anyone die during dinner.'

She snorts, clinks her glass against mine and says, 'I'm adding this to the list of worst first dates I've ever had.'

I don't point out that it wasn't a date. Mostly because I don't want to hear her say it either.

CHAPTER SEVEN

Layla

I HAVEN'T WORN heels this high since... I can't remember. *Have* I ever worn them at all? In a life spent in sensible sneakers and Crocs, I'm not sure I can recall a moment where my feet have felt this constraint. And of course, it was only when I stepped out into the living room with Marina already waiting that I realised my mistake. Because unlike me, Marina is wearing a pair of ballerina slippers. Which makes so much more sense if you think about it. Why have I pressed my poor toes into this unnatural position when flat but elegant shoes exist?

The moment I see Marina, all thoughts about my feet leave my brain. I can only focus on her—scanning her from head to toe as if a higher power compels me to. She's wearing a suit that has to be tailored for her specifically, the jacket sitting snug around her waist and then flaring out just enough to give onlookers a hint of her waist. It's the same suit she wears for all formal occasions and something about the garment seems to bring the same reaction from me every time I see her. Raised pulse, sweaty palms, dry mouth.

It's odd; I've seen her in much more casual dress. Scrubs, pyjamas, workout clothes. Yet it's the dark blue suit clinging to her like a second skin that's making my brain malfunction in a way it shouldn't. I mean, of course I *know* Marina is attractive. Anyone with eyes would know that, and anyone not willing to admit it is a dirty liar. I won't take any questions on that.

What I struggle with is my body's reaction to her—a thing that's only got more complicated as our ruse goes on. I don't know if I can keep blaming our prolonged proximity. I have lived with other people before without feeling like this. And since I've never been with anyone *physically*, I don't know what's normal and what's made up in my head.

The declaration of intent expired a few days ago and on the same day we went to the civil office again with two witnesses—Giuseppe, Marina's lawyer, and, surprisingly enough, Tiziana agreed to stand as the other witness—to sign our official marriage papers. As of last Thursday, Marina and I have been officially married to each other.

The 'wedding' was a rather sombre occasion.

We were escorted into a small meeting room with an official from the civil office, who oversaw us signing the papers one by one, and that was it. I don't know what else I expected in the situation, but it was a lot less…grand? Not that it *needed* to be grand. It wasn't a wedding, just a clerical necessity for us to receive those papers.

She even bought two plain gold bands to sell the fantasy of our union. Thankfully, as doctors, we have a good excuse not to wear any jewellery while we work, but for the event tonight I decided to slip the ring on my finger—trying my best to ignore how *wrong* it felt.

But dressed up the way we are for tonight's event, it seemed odd not to put it on. Invite too many questions from people I don't know but am trying to impress.

'Are you ready to go?' Marina asks, shaking me out of my stupor of admiring her. It's a state of mind I'm slipping into far too frequently, and I need to get a grip on it. I absolutely can't let this attraction grow into anything more when our relationship is based purely on deception. Could anything genuine ever grow out of that?

'Yes,' I say, then I hover at the door as Marina gives the babysitter some instructions about Luca. I surprise myself when I understand maybe a quarter of what they say.

Outside of having regular 'getting to know each

other' coffee breaks during work, Marina has also helped me with my Italian. It's not a language I wanted to learn initially, but after spending some hours in different adoption rabbit holes, I realised the more it looks like I'm integrating, the less likely officials are to be suspicious. And I want to give them exactly zero reasons to come digging.

We have our home visit assessment in a few days, where someone from the Italian agency is coming over to interview us and tour the flat to make sure this is a suitable home for a child. I'm not worried about that, but rather about the many intrusive questions they will no doubt ask.

When Marina finishes up with the babysitter she turns to me, and when she holds out her arm for me to take I catch the flash of gold shining as light bounces off her wedding band. My instinct to wear it was right, but I'm still thrown by how seeing it on her finger makes me feel.

How feeling her hand on my arm sends a herd of invisible tiny horses galloping through my chest to the point where I'm sure an ECG would alert me to a potential cardiac event.

She leads me outside, where a car—including a driver—waits for us. I send her a tight smile when she opens the door for me. My heart races for the mere seconds it takes for her to circle around the car to get to the other side and take her seat next to me. Then the car starts moving towards Catania.

For several minutes—or maybe it's seconds, I'm not really sure—we don't say anything, only the noise of the car's engine filling the air. I glance over at Marina, who is looking ahead. She turns her head when she notices my stare, and the silence veers into awkward.

I don't think we've ever been this quiet with each other. Sure, we've been in the same room in extended silences, like when we're working or sitting on opposite ends of the couch. But it's different now. Not tense…just different? It must be because we're in a new situation.

Not to mention we're now married to each other when just two weeks ago we were merely reluctant co-workers and roommates.

I should say something, right? The whole reason we're going to Catania is for *my* benefit. Sure, showing up as a couple and getting our picture taken in public doesn't hurt, but the real goal is the gala—the kind of event where the right conversation can change everything. If I can corner one of the New Health Frontier directors and make my case for a transfer, maybe I won't be stuck in Sicily forever. A few polite smiles and one perfectly timed pitch could buy me an exit strategy. That's the plan, anyway.

'Thanks for doing this,' I say.

At the same time Marina says, 'You look lovely.'

Heat surges through my body and up to my cheeks, no doubt turning them some shade of blotchy peach or whatever my skin decides looks the least unflattering on me. I don't know what to say in response to the compliment, my brain temporarily disengaged from accessing my speech centre.

Should I tell her she looks flipping gorgeous in this suit? Like to the point that whenever I look at her, my mind drifts off into confusing corners because my fantasies are inappropriate—despite our marital status. Though these particular thoughts cropped up way before we made our deal and my awareness of her in my space went into overdrive.

Thankfully, Marina saves me from my spiralling thoughts when she says, 'Of course, happy to do it.' Her smile softens, but there's a flicker of hesitation in her eyes. 'I know this isn't where you pictured spending the next few months. I wouldn't have asked you to stay if there were any other way.'

'I know,' I say quietly. It's true—Sicily was never the plan. But plans can wait. I could never leave a little boy hanging like that, even if it means my own future is disrupted for the time being. Plus, as much as I want to leave, I haven't secured my transfer. And I might not for a while. Wanting to leave isn't enough to make it happen.

'This doesn't change anything. I'll still talk to the NHF team about my reassignment when the time comes. Until then, I can do this—and I want to. For you. For Luca.'

She exhales, the tension leaving her shoulders. 'That's more than enough. I just didn't want you to feel trapped.'

The flutters in my stomach die almost instantly when she says that, a chill washing over me instead. My eyes dart over her face, looking for hurt I already know I won't find there. During one of our 'getting to know you' sessions, I opened up about the circumstances that brought me here—at least to some extent. I told her it wasn't my first pick and that I'm hoping for a reassignment in the near future.

A part of me wanted to tell her everything. Go into detail about my mistreatment by the previous project manager and how he let me take the blame for a bad call he made. Or how the leadership team at New Health Frontier was happy enough to go along with this farce without considering what it might do to my reputation.

But I couldn't let myself say it, too worried about what she might think. What if she thought I was making excuses by blaming someone else?

'I don't want to put you in an awkward position, though,' I say, reiterating what I told her before.

'You're linked with New Health Frontier, and I don't want to cause you or the clinic any drama.'

Marina waves her hand in a throwaway gesture. 'Don't worry about it. It's not like I'm always in agreement with how they run things or particularly invested in their long-term success. I just had access to funding but needed the help of an organisation like theirs to get my clinic going. Our connection is more opportunistic than based on a shared vision. Helping you get the assignment you want is the least I can do, considering how you're helping me.'

I chew on that for a few seconds, hearing the unvarnished practicality in her voice. I assumed she was deeply loyal to the cause, though, now that she's saying it, I don't know why. Somehow, I thought anyone with enough influence would be all bought in to their mission. And to be honest, I am too. It's just this one specific instance where they have wronged me, and now I need someone else's help to make it right.

Marina has agreed to advocate for me at this New Health Frontier dinner they're hosting in Catania tonight and has invited me along.

I should leave it at that. Still, curiosity gnaws at me hard enough that I blurt out, 'If you're not invested in their success, why not run the clinic independently? You're good at this. I mean, you could have done it on your own.'

Marina's eyebrows rise, almost as if the question surprises her. She looks out of the window and then back at me. 'You'd be surprised by the amount of red tape I encountered when pursuing this idea. There's so much to think about on a legislative, administrative and social impact level. All things I honestly have no clue about. I'm a doctor. I know how to fix people up, but I don't know the first thing about the permits I need to lease a clinic or help asylum seekers without documentation.'

She gives a quick sideways smile before continuing. 'New Health Frontier does most of the heavy lifting with the paperwork and oversight. They shared the knowledge they have since they run clinics like mine all over the world. But I didn't want to cede my independence; we found a more beneficial arrangement. I get to make use of their expertise and infrastructure, and they get to include my clinic's stats in their impact reports without having to pay for any of it.'

My eyes go wide. 'They don't pay for it? Who does?'

Marina doesn't answer right away, and I can tell she's making a decision. There's a subtle shift in her jaw, the way her hand folds in her lap, like she's bracing for a punch that probably won't land.

'I do,' she says.

I blink. 'You—wait. You fund the clinic yourself?'

She nods, her eyes not quite on me. 'Not all of it. There's some grant money—municipal, EU, the occasional private donor. But the building, the initial capital, the equipment is all under a trust I set up a few years ago. When I received the money, I initially didn't know what to do with it, but I knew it needed to go to something worthwhile. To…cleanse it.' She stops, and I realise for the first time how much I don't know about her. *Cleanse it?*

This is…not how people with ordinary backgrounds talk.

It's not my place to pry, not when Marina's been nothing but honest with me, but the silence after she says 'cleanse it' is so dense I can't breathe through it. My curiosity ratchets up a notch; I have to know.

'Cleanse it of what?' I ask.

She doesn't answer right away, her gaze fixed on the darkening landscape beyond the glass. The car rounds a bend, and for a moment the lights of Catania glitter on the horizon. I think she's going to deflect, maybe tell me a story about a dead aunt or a lottery ticket, but instead she says, 'From how I received it. A settlement case from my old hospital. Enough money to start a new life somewhere else—and buy my silence.'

The words hit me harder than I expected, like a rogue blood pressure cuff suddenly inflating around my chest. I try to process what she said, but the first thing my brain does is fill in the blanks with my own assumptions—some shadowy hospital conspiracy, a patient complaint, maybe some botched clinical trial. But the way she said 'buy my silence' is too familiar for it to be something so pedestrian. Did she take the fall for something, too?

'They paid you off to keep you from talking about…?' I let the sentence trail because I can't imagine what a woman like Marina would need to be silenced about. She's a fantastic doctor; I can't imagine anything happening to her integrity.

She breathes in sharp, like I've pressed on a bruise. 'It's not as dramatic as it sounds,' she says, which I can tell is a lie. If it wasn't dramatic she wouldn't be telling me now, in a car on a deserted stretch of Sicilian road, with the city lights still far off. 'It was a harassment claim. Against one of the department heads at my old hospital.' Her jaw tightens, and something behind her eyes goes stormy for a second. 'She wanted more than I was willing to give. When I made it clear I wasn't interested, she in turn made it clear I'd never get anywhere career-wise in the hospital—or Milan for that matter—if I didn't…' she waves her hand through the air, a gesture so unlike her it instantly reads as distress '…"play the game", I suppose.'

I go cold all over. 'That's horrible.'

I mean to say more—ask if the hospital ever even bothered to protect her, or if this settlement was just a tidy way of shooing the problem out of the emergency exit. But Marina talks over the gap, voice a little tighter. 'Once it started, it didn't *stop.* It wasn't just the department head. No one was interested in taking my side. The money was meant to expedite my departure and sweep everything under a rug so thick with secrets you could hide a whole city under it.' She laughs, but the sound has an edge to it. 'I decided the best revenge was to use the money for good. Sometimes I pretend it came from a fairy godmother, but then I remember where it actually came from and it makes me work even harder to justify it.'

I don't know what to say. And because of that, my body moves on its own. Her hand is surprisingly cold to the touch as I wrap my fingers around hers and give it a squeeze. Her head whips up, not having expected the touch, but she doesn't pull away. No, she shifts her hand until our palms press against each other.

A shiver cascades through me, and I'm fighting the feeling even as I yearn to lean into it more. Getting to know Marina has been necessary for our ruse to work, but all the information I keep unearthing—the things she volunteers as if she wants me to know them for other reasons than just our fake marriage—makes it hard to remember this connection isn't real.

That I would be wasting my time wanting anything more than what we have. In a few months, once the dust around the adoption has settled, I hope to be on my way elsewhere, and this thing with Marina in Sicily will have been no more than another chapter.

Not a permanent fixture in my life.

We're both quiet for a stretch, the city's sodium glow slowly brightening and swallowing the last scraps of rural dark. Our hands stay tangled in each other until we reach the venue.

The ballroom is a high-gloss affair: marble floors that threaten to swallow my reflection whole, twin staircases coiling up to a mezzanine choked with topiary, the ceiling crowded with enough crystal to bankrupt a mid-sized nation. The whole thing smells of expensive cologne and gives me a new flavour of anxiety. I don't think I've ever been to such a fancy event in my entire life.

The gala is a fundraiser for New Health Frontier, where they invite their top donors and other important figures to show them how they're spending their money. Though from the size of the venue, I'm guessing most of the money goes into this event.

Next to me, I sense Marina pause, no doubt taking in all the grandeur as well. I'd love to get lost in it if there wasn't this incessant voice at the back of my mind telling me this could be money spent on a clinic or some field medicine operations that actually need it. Aren't the top donors rich people already? Why do they need such an event?

'Well, this isn't what I expected,' Marina says next to me, the distaste in her voice clear. 'I could double the size of the clinic with what it costs to rent this place.'

We pass a string quartet angled just so between the staircases, working their way through something that sounds suspiciously like the soundtrack to *Bridgerton*. The music helps somehow. Makes it easier to walk slowly, to let Marina's hand rest at my lower back in a way that is probably for show but could just as easily be for balance. She keeps the touch there until we reach the main room, where the air changes: heavier, denser, crowded with people who are here for the food and the conversation, not the medicine.

A man in a suit that looks more expensive than my medical degree materialises from behind a column and greets us in a baritone rumble. His hair is so artfully silver I'm stuck wondering if he dyed it this colour, but he bows to Marina and says, 'Dottoressa Moretti, you grace us with your presence,' before turning his gaze to me.

'And this is my wife, Dr Layla Sabri,' Marina says, the words smooth, and yet I feel them ripple across my body. For a second, I hear nothing but the phrase—*my wife, my wife, my wife*—echoing in my head with the urgent repetition of a skipped heartbeat.

I almost miss my cue, but recover with a nod and a, '*Piacere*,' which I hope doesn't sound like I completely butchered it. My Italian still has a lot of room for improvement.

The man—Gio, some grand vizier of regional health, if the lapel pin of the Italian flag and the deference of nearby guests are anything to go by—smiles wider. 'The pleasure is mine,' he says, and his handshake is bone-crushing. I want to glance at Marina to see if she's proud or embarrassed by my performance, but I can't risk looking insecure.

'I was just talking to someone from your organisation about how lucky we are to have you here taking care of things. To think we've got such tremendous talent all the way from Milan,' Gio says, and I feel Marina's fingers twitch at my back. Why is he seemingly sucking up to her? Or is this some veiled insult?

It's the first time I remember seeing Marina

visibly bristle, her posture going just a fraction rigid beside me. In the car, she said her departure from Milan was 'expedited' by the payout, and I wonder now if this man is a part of the machinery that moved her out.

I shake Gio's hand, noting the way his gaze lingers a little too long on our wedding rings. 'I work with Marina in the clinic and we're both very glad to be here,' I say, collecting my most professional tone.

He seems like he's about to probe further, but suddenly a dark-suited assistant materialises at his elbow, whispering something urgent in his ear. Gio's face shifts, and then he's patting Marina once on the arm in a gesture that hovers between old-world warmth and Mafia threat, and says, '*Dottoressa*, we should catch up. You and your lovely wife must join me at my table later. I insist.'

'We'd be honoured,' Marina replies, with a polish so smooth I almost believe her.

'He's more dangerous than he looks, isn't he?' I murmur as we slide through the crowd towards one of the many bars scattered throughout the room. 'He's from the government?'

'I think you could drop him in a tank with live piranhas and he'd come out wearing a new suit,' Marina mutters back, her lips barely moving. 'At the hospital in Milan we dealt with a lot of government funding, so Gio was a regular guest there. Him and Francesca interacted a lot, so I'm…familiar with him.'

Francesca. The name of her ex-whatever. Girlfriend? Marina didn't specify when she spoke about the experience at her last hospital, and I really shouldn't be as curious about it as I am. I'm almost certain she didn't mean to share as much as she has, but then why did she say anything? I've never known her to wear her heart on her sleeve.

'I'll help you avoid him for the rest of the night,' I say, leaning into her side in my role as the doting wife. Her hand slips from my lower back onto my waist, pressing me closer.

It's like the entire side of my body erupts with fire. It's the only way I can explain the heat expanding across my skin and the light-headedness taking me. I lose the thread of my own thoughts as Marina orders us sparkling water from the bar, her fingers still not leaving my waist. Maybe she's leaning harder into the ruse for effect, or maybe she just doesn't want to risk anyone seeing us slip up. I take the glass from her hand and our fingers brush for a split-second—another electric explosion I pretend not to notice, except it leaves my own grip unsteady enough that I have to recover by hiding behind a hasty sip.

'I should be the one helping you today,' Marina says, taking a sip from her own glass. I watch with far too much intent how her throat bobs with each swallow. 'The general secretary of New Health Frontier is currently surrounded by some donors, but the moment we see him break away, I say we pounce. Outside of talking you up and putting your name on his radar, we don't really have much else to do here. The sooner we do that the sooner we can get to the hotel.'

My throat does something weird when she says the word *hotel*, like it kind of constricts. It's another element of the night I hadn't thought about, choosing to deal with it when it's right in front of me instead. Because we only have one room. When booking, Marina offered to get separate rooms for my comfort—since there's nothing that can rattle her—but I declined.

What if we bumped into someone from the event in the lobby? How weird would it be for spouses to have separate rooms? The risk was slim, but when it comes to Luca, I'm not prepared to take *any* avoidable risks.

'Okay, so we're waiting to talk to Mr Nasser and then we're good,' I recap for my benefit rather than hers. 'I imagine he'll be quite busy greeting guests, so we might be a while. What do you want to do until then?'

Marina's grip around my waist loosens as she turns to look at me directly. She's wearing her usual stern expression, but there's a softness around her eyes I'm becoming more familiar with every day. 'We might as well take advantage of the free refreshments and make this an impromptu date.'

She means a platonic date, I tell myself when my heart skips a beat and then accelerates into a gallop. The way you go on a date with a friend who you're committing marriage fraud with, not a real date. The fancy surroundings and the tight suit are throwing me off—making me think of things I shouldn't.

'You also look nice,' I blurt out, giving my confused thoughts full rein to tumble out of my mouth. *Real smooth, Layla.* Marina's hand slackens again, and I can feel the shock my spontaneous declaration caused her. 'Because in the car you said I looked nice, and I didn't say it back, but I meant to. Since, you know, I think you look so chic in your suit,' I add, trying not to cringe. Pretty sure that by trying to explain myself I actually made it so much worse.

The jumble of thoughts scatters when Marina smiles. 'Let's find a quiet corner for a bit. There are a few things I want to know before we talk to Mr Nasser.'

CHAPTER EIGHT

Marina

AFTER CIRCLING THE ballroom twice looking for a quiet place, we step onto the balcony. The sun is long gone, but the air still holds the lingering warmth from a hot day. Or maybe it's all me. Having Layla pressed up into my side is doing things to me I thought would be far easier to control than they are.

Is it because since leaving Milan behind, I haven't been with anyone even on a casual level? At the beginning, the clinic was my entire focus, not letting me think about anything else. Then Agron and Luca came into my life, and I've never wanted for more. Never yearned for a woman's touch this entire time.

Until Layla. Now it feels like my body is charged with a restless energy the moment she looks at me, making it impossible to think clearly whenever I'm close to her. She's not even touching me—I'm the one doing it all—and yet I'm reacting to it all. To the shape of her body pressed into my side, the wafts of her perfume surrounding me, the way the dress hugs her in ways that make my imagination go haywire.

My stomach plummets when she winds herself out of my grasp. We've not even spent an hour playing at being a couple and somehow I'm already used to it. She leans against the balustrade, looking up into the sky, and as my eyes trace the delicate curve of her throat, I get the urge to run my tongue along it to figure out what she would taste like. Would it be as sweet as her scent?

'What do you think about the event so far?' I ask, mainly to distract myself but also because I want to know what she's thinking. That's becoming more of a motivator for me, which is just as bad as yearning to taste her.

No, it's worse. I can explain away attraction and sex and giving in to the need for some closeness. But wanting to know what someone else thinks and feels? It's harder to pretend that it doesn't mean anything. That it's not escalating.

'They really went all out with the venue,' Layla says, turning around and leaning against the balustrade so she's looking back through the doors. I follow suit, leaving enough space between us for it to be decent and feeling every centimetre of separation tug at my core.

'Yeah, it's mostly a spectacle for donors. I've

never felt compelled to show up to one of these. Charming important people isn't where my strengths lie.' I wave towards the door, the crowd far enough away that the noise is dampened, and we can hear the buzz of the city reach us on the balcony.

Layla hums, the vibration filling the air. 'I get it's glamorous and probably something mega donors are used to when they link themselves to such causes. But I don't know… It feels so…'

'Excessive?' I ask when her voice trails off and she nods, her earrings sparkling as they catch the dim light on the balcony.

I allow my eyes to travel downward when I know I shouldn't.

Her dress is simple by the standards of this place, but it does something to me anyway. Midnight blue, high-necked and long-sleeved, the fabric skims her frame like it was tailored with reverence—modest in design, but impossible to ignore. The skirt flows to her ankles in a soft A-line, catching the breeze just enough to move like water. And there, at her wrists and collarbone, the faintest embroidery—silver thread, maybe, or something that glimmers like starlight when it catches the light.

It's the kind of dress that doesn't beg for attention but demands it anyway. From me, but I'm pretty sure I can't be alone in this. Anyone with eyes would notice Layla immediately. How could they not?

'Yes! Everything is so extra. Like, these people donate a lot of money to help people in need. Wouldn't they want every single *dinar* to go towards the organisation? Surely these people can afford their own wine?' Layla waves her hand through the air as she goes on, the passion in her voice so clear—admirable.

I know from previous conversations that she's driven by the need to do good, though we've never reached the point where she told me why or if there were any particular moments in her life inspiring her to give so much of herself. At her age I was just getting involved with Francesca and enjoying the attention that came from being in the line of sight of someone so senior. The memory still sits like grit beneath my skin. I can't be like her; I refuse. But the warmth that flickers whenever Layla smiles gets harder to fight off. It feels both dangerous and undeserved.

I want to know more but, even with the pretence of our fake marriage, I'm not sure I should ask. We only really need to know enough about each other to fool the authorities. So instead, I ask, '*Dinar?*'

Layla lets out a laugh and even in the dim light out here I can see colour rising in her cheeks.

My fingers tingle with the need to reach out and feel the heat on her skin. 'That's the Algerian currency. I guess I should say euro, would make more sense.'

'Do you miss being in Algiers at all? It must be some time since you've been back if you came here straight from your previous assignment.' She's spoken about Algeria before, but whenever she has, it's felt…theoretical? Like she's reciting something from a travel guide rather than sharing her experience. There were some anecdotes from her childhood, just to cover ourselves should there be any questions, but my need to know more about her grows every day.

And it's a need purely inspired by what I want—not what is necessary for our ruse.

Something in her face dims, and it's gone so fast I barely register it, leaving me to wonder what it was about. 'Sometimes? I think I was really keen to leave and see some of the world, but I didn't want to be frivolous about my education either. It took my parents a lot of patience and money to get me through medical school and at times I felt ungrateful to leave like that the moment I was done with my education. Especially for my mother, who did so much to get me to where I'm at now.'

Layla runs her flat palm along the balustrade, eyes cast down.

'Your parents wanted you to stick around?' I ask, and there's an extended pause before she nods.

'My father specifically. He's a doctor too, and he has very specific ideas about how my career should develop,' she says with a mirthless laugh. 'You know, go into family medicine and have a private practice. Sociable hours that still permit a family life. Never mind if I actually want any of these things.'

Something inside me wavers at her last sentence and I can't stop the next question from emerging. 'You don't want a family life?'

Her eyes round, caught off-guard by the question. Which—fair enough. I'm aware of the irony of this, given we are in the middle of faking the thing her father wants for her.

'Well… I haven't put a lot of thought into it, to be honest. So probably, no. I left Algeria not just because I wanted to see what's out there but also to be in a place where I could do the most good. I feel a need that's intrinsic to me to give back. Not everyone has the tools or the freedom to do so, but I do. And I always thought this need and a family don't really complement each other well. Like I'll have to give one up to get the other.'

She twists around to look at me, the light of the balcony catching in her dark brown eyes and giving them a sparkle I haven't seen in them before.

Then again, everything about tonight is different. It's what I focus on when unbidden urges to run my fingers along her cheek bubble up within me.

It's not because I *want* her. No, it's the novelty of the situation. An unexpected byproduct of getting to know someone on a deeper level over a far shorter time than is normal. A side-effect from what we agreed to do.

'Which I know is ironic since now I'm in a situation where I'm doing both. Sort of. The family isn't real, and I still hope to convince New Health Frontier to overturn their decision,' Layla continues, unaware of how her words chip away at something inside me—a new softness that hasn't been there before.

'What happened at your last posting?' I ask, holding onto the first thing I can think of. 'It almost sounds like they banished you here.'

Layla's head dips, a shadow obscuring her eyes so I can't read them. I watch her exhale, a long, controlled breath. For a moment I think she's going to ignore the question, maybe change the subject or make a joke the way she sometimes does to deflect. But instead, she says, very softly, 'I trusted the wrong person, and when they made a critical mistake, they blamed things on me.'

The words hang in the air between us, giving me time to look at them and wrap my head around their meaning. The pain etched into them resonates with me instantly. I've put my trust in the wrong person, and it might have turned out well enough in the long run, but it doesn't erase the struggle. The hurt.

'I was in a field hospital run by New Health Frontier in a conflict zone when a critical patient arrived,' she continues, her gaze now fixed on a point behind me. 'I ordered an airlift for the patient, believing they wouldn't make it through the night otherwise. But my supervisor overruled me. Said the risk to the helicopter crew wasn't justified, that I was exaggerating the symptoms.'

Her jaw flexes, but she doesn't blink. The set of her shoulders is stiff now, like she's bracing for impact. 'We stabilised the patient as best we could, but they deteriorated rapidly. They died before dawn.' She looks up at me then, something unreadable moving behind her eyes. 'Two days later, we found out he was the brother of a regional commander. A very…connected one. Suddenly, there were questions. Meetings. Statements drafted and revised. By the time anyone realised the call hadn't been mine to make, the damage was already done. New Health Frontier needed a clean resolution to present to his family. So they issued a statement saying the airlift had been requested but not pursued. They were… deliberately vague about who made the final call.'

She lets the silence sit there, heavy and deliberate. 'And they reassigned me here, out of the way, to avoid the potential fallout. Like an "out of mind, out of sight" situation. I think it was my supervisor who told the team I'd pushed to call off the airlift, blaming it on my inexperience.' I feel the weight of her words press against me when she shrugs. 'This is why I need someone to help me rehabilitate my reputation. I think I must have some note on my file because whenever I speak to the human resources people at the headquarters, they tell me I'm not eligible for a reassignment. But they can never tell me why.'

This shouldn't bother me in the slightest. I know the people who come here—including Layla—are a fleeting addition to my life. They're here because I need help covering the clinic and I have an agreement with New Health Frontier about funding. It hasn't got to me in the past when young doctors and nurses coming here speak about the clinic and their placement here as a stepping stone. I'm glad for the help and to teach them along the way.

But Layla's words burrow deeper than they should, dislodging something inside me. She must have seen it on my face, for she adds, 'Of course that's not to say I haven't enjoyed my time here or that I'm looking to leave any time soon. These conversations I have are very much future ideas.

I'm committed to seeing this through with you and Luca.'

My breath catches. I don't know if it's the gentleness in her voice or the mention of Luca—like she's not just committed to the plan but to us, to the life we've cobbled together under false pretences. And yet, it doesn't *feel* false. Not when she says it like that.

The weight in my chest shifts. Something warm, uncomfortable, and dizzyingly close to longing swells in its place.

'I know this isn't exactly what you signed up for,' I say, my voice quieter than I intended. 'This place, this situation…me. I know I'm not easy.'

Layla turns towards me again. 'No, but it *is* easy. I was in an odd place when I arrived here, and you gave me the space and time to figure myself out. Let me into the life of your son, who I now adore so much. It was a no-brainer for me to extend the same help. Honestly, I wish you'd been the supervisor on my first placement, because it would have turned out so different.' She pauses to chuckle. 'I'm grateful for the soft landing you gave me without even knowing. And I'm sorry I didn't tell you earlier about all this. It's a…sore spot. But I know now I'm safe with you.'

Her words knock something loose inside me. *Safe.* Throughout my life, I've heard how I'm too severe. How I'm too rigid and tense. Back in

Milan, I thought I had found someone to appreciate this part of me. Someone older, who had more life experience and could appreciate my nature. But things with Francesca had always been more physical, and when that hadn't been enough for me, she'd turned on me.

I've been called inflexible. Boring. Dependable was the most flattering.

Safe.

It's so simple, and yet it feels like a viewpoint so unique to Layla. Like she looks at me and sees not just my actions but my intentions. Who I *want* to be to the important people in my life. Who I want to be to her. And for the first time in a long time, I want to be seen. Not as the clinic director or the woman who poured her payout into a crumbling building out of sheer spite and stubbornness. But as someone who feels all of it—the guilt, the hope, the fear of wanting again.

The space between us feels like a live wire.

I take a step forward, not quite touching but close enough to breathe her in again. 'You can't say things like that to me,' I say, my eyes roaming over her face—searching for a specific signal. A spark or a twitch that tells me—

Layla looks down at the floor for a second, and when our gazes meet again she's peeking through her lashes at me. Her lips part just slightly, and the corner of her mouth lifts—slow, deliberate, like she knows exactly what she's doing. She presses her palm lightly to the balustrade beside my hand, close enough that our fingers almost brush.

She doesn't say anything at first. Just tilts her head a little, smile deepening, and my pulse picks up speed. There's no way I'm imagining the tension snapping into place.

Her next words spell my ruin. 'Tell me to stop, and I will.'

Stop. I think it, but the words refuse to cross my lips. My body has taken over, more than happy to kick my sense of self-preservation to the side for this one moment. Deep in the recesses of my brain, I know what I'm about to do is the dumbest thing I *can* do. It'll make an already fraught situation so much more complicated. But I can't stop—don't *want* to. Not when this gorgeous woman looks up at me like that, eyelashes feathering over her cheeks with every blink. Telling me she wants it, too.

How can I resist when her draw is so foreign, so novel? I'm not sure I wouldn't be missing the opportunity of a lifetime—however long that might last.

I slide my hand towards hers until there's no more space between us on the balustrade. My fingers weave through hers without meeting resistance from Layla. No, she keeps looking at me with a spark in those big brown eyes that tightens my core. She exhales when I take another step closer, tilting her head back when our fronts meet.

Having had her pressed against my side tested my willpower earlier. But the sensation was nothing compared to what rocks through my body now. I lean down, crowding her space, and for a second there's nothing except the hummingbird thrum in my chest and the taste of her anticipation on the air. I've kissed before—plenty—but not like this. Never with my whole body wound tight around the possibility that if I do it wrong, the world could end. That tonight will be a story we never tell anyone, not even ourselves.

But then it's just us. Layla and me. No audience, no expectations, just the shared illusion of heat and gravity. I press my lips to hers. She exhales into my mouth, and I inhale her, famished. If she's surprised by how much I want her, she doesn't show it—instead, she melts into me, her hands coming up to cradle my jaw.

The kiss is warm and slow, almost careful, but there's a deeper hunger at its edge. I can taste the wine from her dinner, and something else, spicy and wild—her. The suppression of need, the effort to keep still, only feeds the fire.

For a tiny eternity, we balance on the crest between want and have, suspended by the close, steady press of our bodies and the undeniable evidence of something shared. Neither of us wants to be the first to let go.

But it's Layla who moves first. Her hand finds the back of my neck, fingers threading through the hair I tried so hard to tame tonight, and she draws me closer, deepening the kiss in a way that catches me completely off-guard. My pulse stutters, then surges. I'm not sure if I'm holding her up or if she's keeping me from sliding to the floor. All I know is that the balcony, the ballroom, the entire churning mess of my life shrinks to a pinpoint with her body pressed flush to mine.

I let myself sink into it. Maybe, in another life, I would have been bolder about this. Maybe I wouldn't have needed the safety of darkness or the pretext of performance to let myself reach for what I want.

It's a minor miracle that I don't shatter into pieces when the doors behind us swing open and voices bellow out onto the balcony. I'm still tangled with her—lips, fingers, breath—when her body stiffens, heartbeat jack-hammering against mine. For a fraction of a second, I taste nothing but the ozone of panic. Then we break apart.

'I told you the view was better from this side,' says a voice I know immediately—Mr Nasser, the general secretary. The man we're here to speak to so he can clear Layla's name and get her reassigned to a different place. A place that's not here, in my house. Next to me. Because she doesn't want to be here.

The thought is a potent ice blast to the fire that caught inside me just a few moments ago.

I do my best to swallow what's left of my heart, which is currently somewhere around my ankles, and take the opportunity to step a polite distance away from Layla. It doesn't matter that my body feels hollowed out, or that my lips still burn with the memory of hers. What matters is that this is a professional event, and the general secretary of New Health Frontier is here, and if I ever want a future for the clinic—and for Luca—I need to keep it together.

'Mr Nasser,' I say, smoothing my hair and plucking the last shreds of composure from the night air. 'We were hoping to speak to you this evening.' I don't trust myself to look at Layla, so I don't. 'I'm Marina Moretti and I run a clinic affiliated with New Health Frontier here on Sicily. This is my wife, Dr Sabri.'

He's shorter than I expected, with a quickness in his gaze that makes me instantly grateful for the time Layla and I spent memorising our backstory. He shakes my hand, then hers, with a pleasant firmness.

'A pleasure to meet you, Dr Moretti, Dr Sabri. Thank you for joining us tonight. I'm always keen to hear from the bright doctors who join our causc. They make much more interesting company than donors.'

We fall into the usual small-talk pleasantries—the thank-yous, the compliments on the venue, the polite nods towards donors—yet every word feels oddly dissonant. My mind is still back there on the balcony rail, with the taste of Layla's mouth lingering like a secret I can't swallow. She stands just close enough that I can sense her warmth, the faint brush of her sleeve against mine, and it sharpens my awareness of her to an almost unbearable pitch. Even as I smile and keep the conversation smooth, part of me is reeling, caught between the echo of her lips and the danger of being caught out.

I steer the topic where I need it to go.

'Dr Sabri has been an incredible addition to the clinic,' I say, careful to pitch my tone just right—admiring without overplaying it. 'Her experience in field hospitals has been invaluable, but she deserves to be back in a post where she can use her skills to their fullest. She's been hoping for another placement soon.'

Nasser's sharp eyes flick between us, and I can almost hear the gears turning in his head. 'Oh? Someone told me you got married a few weeks ago—is that right? Why leave so soon when you two just found each other? You wouldn't want to remain close to your wife?' he asks, eyes landing on Layla.

She freezes. I see it in the second lift of her shoulders, the way her mouth opens, but no sound comes out.

I lean in before the silence can stretch. 'Because our marriage isn't the kind that buckles at distance,' I say, hoping he believes me. 'We're committed to making it work, whatever it takes. Even if it means long flights, different time zones. Our work is important, and so are we. We don't see those as contradictory.'

Nasser studies me for a long moment. Then his lips quirk into something like approval. 'That kind of commitment is rare,' he says. 'Well, if you encounter any trouble, get in touch with my office and they'll see what they can do.'

Relief loosens something tight in my chest, but it doesn't erase the pulse of awareness still running between Layla and me. Nasser drifts into a story about a donor who once tried to expense a private jet to bring a giraffe to a field hospital—'for the children, you see'—and while I manage the appropriate smiles, I can tell Layla is still caught in the after-image of what just happened. Her eyes are wide, blinking a bit more than normal, and the tips of her ears are blushing the same deep red as the sky over the city. When Nasser's phone buzzes and he steps away to answer it,

I seize the opportunity to gently touch Layla's elbow. She flinches, the contact electric, but lets me steer her down the balcony steps and into the less crowded annexe just off the main ballroom.

CHAPTER NINE

Layla

THIS IS STUPID. *I'm* being stupid, right?

After speaking to Mr Nasser and getting such a positive response—plus his business card—my mind went straight into overdrive imagining where I might go next once I've done my part in helping Marina with Luca. Only the daydreaming didn't last long because the moment *any* thought becomes about Marina, I fall down the inevitable pit of 'things I didn't realise I felt for Marina that are now just living down here in the darkness'.

It's not a good place to be in—and that's because it's a *great* place to be in. Everything about Marina is amazing, and now, knowing what her mouth tastes like, or what she feels like pressed close against me, is just adding to the pile of things. Which would be all well and good if this were something that could happen. If we could be a thing.

We can't. The thought alone clashes with the

vision of the future I have dreamed up. Marina has her whole life—her son, hcr clinic—here in Sicily, and all I want is to be somewhere else.

It *is* still what I want, right? The only reason I'm hesitating is because when I think about it, Marina is the only thing that pops into my head. Big and looming and deliciously seductive.

And it's those disruptive thoughts that lead me to this moment, making me doubt if I'm walking down a sane path or if the impromptu make-out session earlier has scrambled my brain so hard I'm beyond redemption.

Because I'm sitting on the bed in my underwear, waiting for Marina to come out of the bathroom. We didn't linger long after the conversation with Nasser, since we'd achieved our goal and Marina wanted to avoid potentially running into other people from her old life. So we headed for the hotel, which was only a short walk away—one we did in silence. I tried to bring up the kiss, needing to know what it meant. Or if she felt the same way as I did. Even after Nasser's interruption, my heart hasn't calmed down. Neither has the fire she ignited in me. It's been crawling through me for hours now, latching on to anything it can use as fuel.

My problem is—I've never done this before. I've never seduced anyone in my life. Have never crossed that line into intimacy before. It's not something I ever considered outside the context of marriage, and now…well, I *am* technically married to the woman I desire. Though part of me knows I'm telling myself that to justify my feelings.

This attraction has billowed into something far larger than I could have anticipated, and I have an inkling it was the same for Marina. Well, a bit more than just a hint, considering she was the one to approach me and initiate that first kiss.

I shudder, my stomach swooping through my body, and even though the air is balmy in the hotel room I feel my nipples strain against the fabric of my bra. Wait, should I take it off? No, that would be too forward, right? Regardless of how I *think* she feels, I don't have any confirmation until she actually says it.

Leaning back, I stretch my arms behind me to prop myself up on the bed. My long legs dangle off the edge, and I cross them. Then I uncross them. Maybe tugging them underneath me looks better? Oh gosh, how do people do this? In quiet moments, whenever I thought about what it would be like to lie in bed and wait for my future spouse, there wasn't such an air of…awkwardness.

Then again, it's my fantasy, so I get to pretend I'm not the inexperienced mess I am. But the thing is, even though I've never done this before, I know I want to. With Marina. I want to be more. It's a dangerous thing to want, I know that. With our agreement and the fake marriage and Luca in the picture, it feels like our future's already been decided. She's built her life here, and I yearn to find something out there, cut my teeth in the field hospitals out there and make a career out of it. Show my parents I'm meant to be more than a family doctor—a wife.

But even as I try to tell myself it's hopeless, there's a side of me that keeps thinking back to every moment Marina opened up to me. How she told me about her ex harassing her and her decision to use the money from the settlement to give back. Do good. It's the same need I have pulsing through me and what inspired me to join New Health Frontier in the first place. In that regard, we're the same. It's our actions that differ, but at the core of it all, we want the same thing. We...match.

How am I supposed to leave someone like her and not feel it all the time, for the rest of my life?

A hairdryer whines into silence in the bathroom and I try to strike a natural pose, but every possible arrangement of my limbs just feels like a parody of seduction, or a joke that somehow got out of hand. Too awkward. Too obvious. Not enough. I try not to spiral, but my body's already ahead of me, heart fluttering so hard in my ribs that I wonder if she'll notice it the moment she comes out.

I try for 'hot and mysterious' and end up looking like a stunned bird, perched at the edge of the hotel bed, knees together, ankles crossed, gaze fixed on the television looping muted footage of some Sicilian cooking show. In my peripheral vision, I track the shifting light under the bathroom door. A soft click, and then Marina steps out, towel knotted around her torso.

She pauses when she sees me, standing just inside the bathroom door, bare feet on the tiles and a triangle of yellow light sharpening her outline. Her gaze slides over me and all up my body, lingering everywhere I'm most worried about, but it's not a critical or even clinical kind of looking. There's a pause, a shift in her stance, and then something like heat passes across her face. My heart leaps.

She's so beautiful like this, stripped of her usual composure and just a little bit stunned. Her dark hair is slicked back and still wet, exposing her sharp cheekbones and the elegant line of her jaw. The towel obscures a figure I'm far too familiar with already, but even like this she looks like she's stepped out of a vision and into reality. How can she have such an effect on me when it's all supposed to be fake?

The silence sharpens. The thing about me is

that I am not good with silences. Not on the job, not in life, and definitely not here, where every second is a chance for the doubt in my head to get louder. I want to say something—make a flirty joke, or even a bad one like asking if she needs the remote, or just, I don't know, say her name. But nothing comes out. The air between us is thick with whatever has been building all night, and it's clear neither of us is equipped to process it in words.

Her eyes rake down my body, and I see the moment she registers that I am, in fact, waiting for her. That I want her.

'Layla.' Her voice is hoarse, almost pained, and I brace for her to say it was a mistake, that she wants to draw the line again—back to safe, back to professional. But she just stands there, knuckles whitening on the towel, her breath short and shallow. 'This is… You can't do this to me.'

I blink, searching her face for what she really means. I know this is a gamble and with how little I know about, well, seduction, I'm uncertain where the line is. All I see is *her*, trembling slightly—with the effort of keeping herself contained? The way she says it, I think she doesn't want me to stop. She just wants me to know what it's doing to her. How close she is to giving in.

'I'm sorry,' I say, but I stay where I am, rooted

at the end of the bed. 'I can stop if you really want me to.'

She steps forward, the towel making her look even more vulnerable than if she'd walked out naked.

'I shouldn't have kissed you,' she says, each syllable deliberate, 'and I shouldn't have blurred the line between us.' Her mouth is tight, like she's holding in a much larger confession. 'I know what you want. I know what you're after in life, and it's not this.'

I should say something. Reassure her that I'm not falling apart, that I'm not going to crash my entire existence on the rocks because of a single night. But the words don't want to come out. Instead, I just hold her gaze and I don't move. If she wants to walk away, she's going to have to do it. I'm staying right here, making my intentions clear.

'I know you're not looking for anything serious, with Luca and everything. Plus, being married to me can't be something that's a plus in the dating market. And you know I'm yearning for what's out there in the field hospitals.' I pause, unsure where these words are going.

Marina doesn't walk away. No, she steps closer still until I can feel her body heat rippling away from her. She's barely breathing, and the towel at her chest looks one tug away from gravity's surrender. I sit very still, every cell on alert. She stops at the foot of the bed, close enough I can see the quiver in her jaw, the way her pupils are blown wide in the low light.

'I don't want to stop,' she says, voice hoarse and stripped raw, 'but if we continue, I don't know what this turns into. Things can't change between us.' Her mouth tugs into a wry smile, then the veneer crumbles and she is bare, more exposed than I've ever seen her. 'Not for lack of my wanting it. You.'

Her admission detonates something reckless inside me. 'Then don't stop,' I say, my own voice so low I don't recognise it. Nor do I understand the pure want drugging me. 'Please.'

She drops the towel. My brain stutters, eyes going wide as I take her in. I'm no stranger to the human body, not after years of med school and triage units. But nothing in those years prepared me for this: the deliberate invitation in the way she lets it fall, the ownership in her stance, the way she looks at me—hungry.

Time slows. My eyes crawl over her perfection, the exact lines of her collarbones, her smooth olive skin still dewed from the heat of the shower. Her hips draw my gaze, the taut belly with the faintest crescent scar slashing across it. I want to press my mouth there and learn what she tastes like, but my body's locked in place, mesmerised and helpless.

Marina takes another step forward, coming to a standstill between my knees. Her thighs brush against mine, and I want to both snap them shut and open wide. The touch is minuscule, but it ricochets through me with a force that takes my breath away.

My pulse is a drumline, racing ahead of whatever rationale might still be left in my head.

'Layla.' Her voice drops lower this time, not trembling at all. 'You're overdressed for this occasion.'

Her hands come down on my thighs as she bends down, fingers splayed so they almost touch the wispy fabric still covering me. My breath hitches. I open my mouth for some retort, but the words tangle and die at the back of my throat when her hands slip up, skimming the outsides of my thighs, then land—hot, deliberate—at my hips. I'm certain she can feel the tremor running through me.

'May I?' she asks, already tracing the elastic at my waistband.

'Yes,' I say, then, because that didn't seem enough, I add, 'please.'

She peels the fabric away, slow enough that it's almost torture. The air feels cooler on my skin, but the burn of her gaze makes it worse…twice as bad, twice as good.

She takes her time looking at me. Not in a way that feels clinical or appraising, but more like she's trying to memorise what's in front of her. I feel her gaze as a physical thing, like the lightest fingertips ghosting over my skin, and it makes me shiver even though she's still inches away. Her lips part as if to say something, but she just shakes her head slightly, a smile flickering at the corner of her mouth.

'What?' I ask, wanting to hear her thoughts. *Any* thoughts, not just right now. That's how obsessed I'm growing with this woman. I want to know what she thinks about current events, what her favourite flavour of gelato is and if pineapple on pizza is as divisive a topic in Italy as it is in the rest of the world.

I also want to feel her hands on me, and I get that wish when her hands move up, bracketing my hips and sliding up across my ribs.

She's careful, almost reverent in the way her hands span my ribs—thumbs brushing under the elastic edge of my bra. Every nerve in my body has tuned itself to her.

'You are so beautiful, Layla,' she says, and it's not so much a compliment as it is a statement of fact, forced out of her like a confession that's been pent up for years. Her hands don't fumble, but her voice does, tripping over the words. 'I know I shouldn't say that, but you feel exactly how I imagined you would. Because I shouldn't actually tell you how many hours I've spent thinking about you.'

She brings her lips to my collarbone, planting a slow, deliberate kiss there, and then another, trailing them across the hollow of my throat the way a cartographer sketches the boundaries of a new and wondrous territory. My palms tingle with the need to touch her, but I keep them pressed against the bed, letting her set the pace.

Marina has far more experience; I have no doubt she will guide me.

Her hands move up, fingers sliding under the straps, and with the gentlest pressure she pulls them off my shoulders. They slither down my arms, bringing the bra cups with them, until the entire thing is hanging loose at my waist. Only then does she pull back enough to look at me again.

It's a bold thing: to be this naked in front of another person and yet not feel even a flicker of shame. I thought I would, having never done that. But need is the only thing pumping through me.

There's no part of this I want to hide from her. Not even the trembling or the scrapes on my shins from the emergency the other day, or even that one awkward mole I used to hate, right below my sternum, which she looks at for a fraction of a second longer than the rest of me.

'You okay?' she asks, voice so low it's almost a rumble, unhooking my bra and peeling away the last layer of fabric. Her hands find my waist again, then softer, the insides of my arms, tracing up to cup my jaw.

I nod, barely able to breathe with how tightly I'm wound. Before I can summon a real answer, her mouth is on mine, hungry in a way that feels weeks in the making—even before we agreed to get closer for our ruse.

Her hands are everywhere: framing my face, pushing a stray curl behind my ear, sliding down along my neck and collarbone, then lower. I seize up, the entire surface of my skin electrified. For someone who zoomed through puberty and never had time for high school make-out sessions, I feel alarmingly out of my depth. Marina's tongue finds mine, and everything in my body unspools so fast my thoughts tumble away, insecurities forgotten.

I let her pin me, not out of passivity but because I crave the intent behind it: her weight, the anchoring pressure of her thigh between mine, the purposeful way her hand slides up to cradle my jaw. We are both steady only because of the other's gravity.

When we kissed on the balcony, I tried to keep

it contained, treat it like a glitch in the matrix. But this dam, now finally breaking? There's no way to hold it back for me. Not when she's filled my head with fantasies since I started living with her. And our approach has been so gradual, the attraction low, simmering and unassuming, that I didn't realise it was on me until our little marriage scheme began. And now it's too late for me to back away from her. Not without losing something that feels like it's part of myself.

Her teeth graze my lower lip, and I gasp. It shocks me how blinding the sensation is—like she's shot a current through my entire body, every molecule jumping to attention. I want to drag her closer, slam our bodies together until there's no space left between us, but she's beating me at my own want.

When we come back for air, Marina's kneeling on the bed, her knees bracketing my thighs. Heat ripples off her skin and over mine, the pressure of her on top of me so delicious, it's hard to breathe.

'Tell me what you want.' Her voice is low as she asks this, framing my face with her hands and gently swiping her thumbs over my cheeks.

'I just want…' I trail off, unsure how to put this into words. My want is an ethereal thing, and every time I try to grasp for it, it comes back in the shape of Marina. 'You.'

Marina smiles, drawing my face closer to press

an unhurried kiss to my lips. It's leisurely, as if time isn't passing outside these four walls and nothing will ever catch up with us. Reality is a loose concept right now. 'I want it to feel good for you. What do you like?'

She kisses me again before I answer, her moan rumbling through my bones and stoking the fire inside me higher. Is this the moment when I tell her about my lack of experience? I hesitate not because I'm ashamed, but rather…what if it bothers her? Whatever this is, we both know it's not permanent. What if she doesn't want an inexperienced lover with uncertain fingers and a clumsy mouth?

Marina straightens, brushing some loose hair from my brow when I don't answer. My heart is beating in my throat as I answer. 'I don't know. I haven't ever…' I let the rest of the sentence hang in the air, too worried I'm ruining my chances of something great with my honesty.

But I should've known I don't need to be worried. Not when it comes to Marina. 'You have never been with a woman?' she asks, nothing but heat and kindness in her voice.

I shake my head. 'Or a man. I just—with all the studying and then working in the field, dating hasn't been at the top of my priority list.'

'I see.' Marina's hand trails down to my neck, her gentle touch sending a shiver through me. I let out a shaky breath when her fingers wander lower, stopping at the swell of my breast. She pauses there, then bends down, and her mouth follows the path her hand has drawn. 'We can figure out what you like, if you want.'

She places a kiss on the top of my breast, her tongue darting out as if to show me what exactly she means by that.

'I want, yes,' I breathe out, and moan when her lips close around my nipple, drawing it into her mouth.

Lightning explodes through me, and my back hollows out as I try to eliminate the distance that doesn't exist between us. Marina is already as close to me as she can be, and somehow it's still not enough. I need more of her mouth, her fingers, her tongue all over me.

'We already know you like this,' Marina says when she lets go of me with a *pop*, but before I can even feel her absence, her hand replaces her mouth and she shifts to my other side. Her attention is intoxicating, showing me a world I didn't realise I had been missing.

Have I, though, or is this something unique to Marina?

'Lie down, love,' Marina says, slipping off the bed and standing in front of me in all her naked glory.

I don't. Instead, I slide closer to the edge of the

bed, my hands finding their way to her hips on their own and pulling her closer until my mouth connects with her skin. Her inhale is sharp, and I feel her muscles contract under my touch when I mimic what she did to me, letting my mouth wander from her navel and up. Somehow my brain shuts off, and I'm thankful for it, because I know I *should* be overthinking this, but I'm not. No, I'm letting my body follow the rhythm of hers as I kiss, lick and suck my way up to her breasts, pulling her closer until we're pressed so tightly together there's no difference between my body and hers.

Marina's hands twine into my hair, and she drags my mouth up to hers. She tastes like toothpaste and wine and something saltier—the taste of my own skin, maybe, from where she pressed her lips before. The thought sends a miniature earthquake through my bones, and I let myself get lost in it, in her.

'You're picking this up so fast,' Marina croons when we split apart, her tongue darting out to lick over my lower lip. 'Let me show you what I've been thinking about doing to you.'

For how long? The question manifests in my mind, but I don't let it slip out. Whether I've just found her in a particularly horny moment or if this is something she's fantasised about the way

I have is irrelevant. It doesn't change anything between us.

Would knowing the answer help?

My thoughts scatter when she pushes her hand down on my sternum, guiding me back onto the bed. Then she kneels down on the floor, her body between my thighs. I feel the soft pressure of her skin on mine as her hands come down on my legs, swiping upwards in lavish strokes. Every time her palm smooths over my side, her thumb drags slow fire behind it. I want to reciprocate, to show her how I feel—how I'm ready to burst—but everything is so new I can barely keep up.

Her hands slip to my inner thighs and, without any pressure, I open wider for her. I expected some shyness to remain, to pull me out of this moment. But when her breath ghosts over my centre, there's nothing but molten fire in my body.

'*Bellissima...*' I know the word, having listened to the native population enough to pick up some useful phrases. But it still hits me in an unexpected place. Beautiful?

How can I have this effect on her? I hear it more than see—her breath hitching, her hands tightening on my thighs. That's what I want, isn't it? To make her feel like she's making me feel? I try to say her name, but it turns into a garbled string of sounds when her fingers reach the apex of my thighs, brushing over me.

Marina parts me, not even pausing before her thumb brushes along my seam. The touch is like a firebrand, searing through me hot enough that I lose control. I buck, almost bowing off the bed, except Marina wraps one arm around me and keeps me in place—and at her will.

'This is how badly you want me, is it?' she mumbles as she keeps teasing me. 'This is…incredible.'

I open my mouth to say something, return her sweet words. Tell her how much this means to me, even though I know I shouldn't. But Marina robs me of any coherent thought again when she says, 'Let me taste you. Please.'

I nod.

My body goes rigid at the sound of her voice. Not just because of what Marina says, but the way she says it. Like she's asking for permission and promising to ruin me at the very same time. If I had any functioning brain cells left, I'd probably overthink the etiquette of all of this: how to hold myself, where to look, whether to let my hands tangle in the sheets or just reach for her again and never let go.

But wanting trumps logic. Wanting trumps everything.

Her mouth finds me in a way that's somehow both gentle and greedy, like she's been starving for this and now she's determined to memorise every detail. I clench the blanket in my fists, trying not to writhe, but she makes it impossible. There is a split second when I worry about doing this right—about making a fool of myself, or making some embarrassing noise—but then the heat of her tongue sweeps every thought out of my head.

Oh. *Oh.*

No one tells you that pleasure can be a kind of panic. That it can set every muscle alight with the urge to run or to scream or to burst into tears. I do none of those things—I just let out a sound that's half-cry, half-laugh, like I'm shocked this is possible. Her hands are locked around my thighs, anchoring me when my hips buck, and for a wild second I wonder if she'll ever let me go or if this is how I'll die: undone, exposed, and completely hers.

'You're so responsive and delicious,' she murmurs, voice muffled, and the vibration of it almost breaks me—like she's inside my chest, not just between my thighs. 'I could eat you out all day and never tire of it.' I whimper. I actually whimper at her words, and bursts of colour appear behind my eyelids.

Thoughts tumble through me, never surfacing enough to manifest. None except one. I want to stay in Sicily and never leave, I think, which is the most deranged thing I could possibly think right now and so, of course, it's true.

It's not because Marina's mouth along with her fingers are coaxing pleasure out of me I never thought possible. No, though I'd be lying if I didn't admit this is exactly what I was imagining with her.

What gets me is how *perfect* this all feels. How predestined.

And Marina...she knows exactly what to do—to slow down and then speed up, to tease and then reward, to coax sensation out of me until I'm begging for more.

When I finally break apart, it's sudden and violent, like someone's detonated the core of me and I'm left to feel the aftershocks. I arch off the bed and cry out a sound I barely recognise as my own. Marina holds on, riding it out with me, never breaking contact, never letting go. I feel myself dissolve, then reassemble, then dissolve again.

For a long time, all I can do is tremble and gasp and say her name, over and over, like a prayer. My brain is melted. My bones are gone. The only thing real is the way her hands stroke along my legs, gentle now, grounding me back into my body. She kisses up my thighs with slow, savouring care, then drags her body up until she's lying next to me.

Pressed against my side, I feel tiredness claw at me almost instantly, but I fight it off.

'I think we figured out at least one thing you like,' Marina says close to my ear. I shiver when she drags her hand across my stomach.

I just manage to fight my heavy limbs and turn to the side to look at her. Our legs interlock, pulling us into a warm embrace that has no business feeling as intimate as it does.

This night is supposed to be an outlier, and yet I want it to be the norm. Do I want it more than getting back into the field? I push the thoughts away, focusing on Marina instead. This night might be a gigantic question mark, but it's far from over.

Her skin pebbles under my fingers, and I let instinct guide me, palm skimming up her side, learning the slope of her waist, the soft give of her. I lean in to kiss the pulse at her throat, and my hand starts to wander—curious, bolder now, hungry to map what she'll let me have.

Marina catches my wrist—not hard, just enough to still me. Her eyes are dark and steady, the corner of her mouth tipping into something that's almost a plea. 'Layla,' she murmurs, voice rough with want and restraint, 'we can take this slow if you don't feel ready.'

I want to, though. I want to make her feel good—maybe desperately so. Not just because she's been so careful with me, but also because this is the first time in my life someone has ever made me feel this way. Seen, wanted, protected. It makes something wild and reckless catch fire inside my chest.

'I'm okay,' I say, catching her hand and holding it right where it is, over my heart. 'I want this, Marina. And I want you to feel as good as you made me feel.'

Marina actually looks surprised. Her eyes widen—a spark flares in them—and then her mouth tips into a smile that is almost shy.

'This isn't some quid pro quo. I wanted to see you unravel and I have. But I'm not expecting anything in return,' she says, but I shake my head before she can start pulling away.

'And now let me learn how good it feels to touch you. Please.' My ears are burning, but I don't look away. 'If tonight is all I get with you, then I want to have it all.'

A beat of silence, and then she exhales, tension leaving her posture as she shifts closer—the hesitation replaced by something more liquid, languid.

'Okay,' she murmurs, voice dropping. She's tucked so close now that her breath ghosts over my cheek, and when I nod, she kisses me—slow, soft, like we're both finding our rhythm for the first time.

I let instinct take over, fingers trailing down

her body again, mapping every curve and hollow with an intensity only matched by my need to get this right. My hand slides up her thigh, not sure if I should go further than that, but the little catch in her breathing tells me I'm not doing anything wrong. Far from it.

Her skin is hotter than mine, muscles taut under my palm. I nuzzle into her neck, emboldened now, and trace my lips along her jaw, then lower, breaking off only to murmur, 'Just tell me if you want me to stop.' The request is almost laughable, considering how she shivers under my touch.

'I won't,' Marina whispers, threading her fingers through my hair—gentle, but with a kind of urgency that makes my pulse jump again. 'Keep going.'

Her hand guides mine and the tension that had my shoulders up around my ears ebbs away. We move carefully, learning each other by centimetres—where she sighs, where she tilts her hips, where a kiss pressed just beneath her ear makes her breath hitch and her fingers tighten in my hair.

'That's it,' Marina murmurs, the words barely sound, more warmth against my mouth than speech. I follow the sound, the warmth, until we're tangled again, foreheads touching, laughter catching between kisses when I fumble my way towards her climax—until it rushes over her.

I don't think about tomorrow, or transfers, or interviews. I think about the shapc of this moment and the way it fits. When Marina's voice breaks on a soft, startled sound, I close my eyes and let the world fall away, following her down into the dark where everything feels easy and true.

CHAPTER TEN

Marina

I'M STARING AT the bowl of biscotti on the coffee table, fixating on the uneven distribution of almonds, when the social worker clears her throat for the fourth time in as many minutes. Layla and I occupy one end of the couch, bodies angled towards the woman in the sensible navy trouser-suit whose feet are firmly planted on my new living room rug, its fibres pristine only because the package arrived less than twenty-four hours ago. I panic-bought it online after reading that social workers are more likely to approve an adoption if the home looks 'well-appointed but unpretentious'.

Luca is in the corner of the room, absently constructing and demolishing a Lego city. He hasn't looked up since the interview began, which I tell myself is a good thing—shows independence, comfort in the space. Layla sits with her hands neatly folded in her lap, every so often uncrossing and recrossing her ankles. Her posture is composed, but the slight quiver at the corner of her mouth betrays a tension not even she can flatten. I'm not faring much better. I've started to bounce my knee, but catch myself and clamp it still every time the social worker's eyes cut my way.

With how messy we've let things get between us since the night in Catania, I'm surprised we're managing to look normal and not like the pile of raging hormones that we are. Which is awkward to admit at my age, but something about Layla gets to me the way little else has in life—to the point where I kissed her.

And then did more than kiss her. Both are mistakes I shouldn't have made. And I know I shouldn't have repeated the kissing and the more when we got home. On the way back, I was ready to tell her this was a one-off thing. Our lives aren't compatible. My entire focus needs to be on Luca and the clinic, while Layla wants to be out there in the field, seeing the world while saving lives.

We should have left it at one night—explained it away as a mistake. Only when we got home we sought each other out again. I can't even remember if it was me who went to her door or if she stood there just as I opened mine. Probably both. We haven't stopped sleeping with each other since.

And now we're at the final checkpoint of the

adoption: an interview with the woman from the *commissione per l'adozione internazionale*. If she issues us a decree of suitability, Giuseppe told me this would be sufficient for the Albanian authorities now that I also have a marriage certificate to show.

The woman—her name is Antonia—clicks her pen and glances at her notes, glasses perched at the end of her nose in a way that's almost caricature. 'Let's talk about routines,' she says, her gaze sweeping first to me, then settling on Layla. 'How do you divide daily responsibilities for Luca? Is there a system, or do you manage tasks as they come?'

'We're both early risers, so usually whoever gets to the kitchen first starts breakfast,' Layla says, and I watch in fascination as she fakes a casual laugh, tucking a strand of hair behind her ear. 'If one of us has a crazy morning at the clinic, the other takes over—sometimes it's a relay. But we eat dinner together every night, no matter what. It's non-negotiable.' When Layla smiles at me, my heart lurches into my throat.

It's not even a lie. The three of us do eat dinner together every night and most of the time Luca demands Layla put him to bed. She started reading him bedtime stories from Algeria, her way of speaking imprinting on him enough that I can sometimes hear it in his pronunciation of words. He's almost developed a French accent now.

'That's excellent,' Antonia says. 'Research shows consistency is a pillar of child development. What about personal struggles? As I understand it, your relationship is still fairly recent. Our most important task here is to ensure Luca grows up in a safe environment.'

Some choice words flash through my head when she says that, mainly how she can say this with a straight face when the alternative is to ship Luca back to some unknown foster family in Albania. Even single and pouring most of my efforts into work, I'm still the superior choice. Not to mention that I love him as if I had birthed him myself.

Layla's warm hand wraps around mine and her thumb brushes across my skin, calming the tempest. She gives me a sidelong glance with a small smile, ever the reassuring presence in my life. I really couldn't have done any of this without her in so many more ways than she knows. It's strange to think that all I wanted from her at the beginning was a signature on a piece of paper, and now…?

I can't let myself go there, or the genuine affection and love I keep buried deep inside me will spill out for her to see. And I can't do that to her when I promised her I would help her reach her goals.

'We may not have been together long, but that doesn't change our commitment to each other or this family,' Layla says when I remain quiet, giving my hand a squeeze.

Right. I should participate in this conversation.

'Yes, we take things one day at a time, like any other couple. But whenever we make any decisions, we always think about what's best for Luca. His life has been traumatic enough with his father's passing, so we're here to provide him with stability.'

Antonia nods, scribbling something on her notepad, and Layla adds, 'That's right. Marina has never made a secret of her commitments, and our relationship will not get in the way of choosing what's best for this family. We both know what the priority here is.'

Her words set something loose inside me—the small kernel of doubt that has been there since the night of the charity dinner. A night where we somehow managed to push the possibility of *us* further away while also bringing it closer than ever.

I know she reached out to Nasser and got his buy-in to 'look into her situation'. We both know the good news is imminent. And I want to be happy for her. I *am*. Because the tiny part of me that wants her to stay—the one that flinches when she says 'we both know what the priority here is'—knows I shouldn't feel this way.

I can't have her. But I also can't stop myself from wishing it was different. And from saying so.

'Every day we're learning how to communicate with each other better. We're used to long shifts and stress, and I'll admit it's a challenge sometimes. But I'm glad to have her by my side as we discover this.'

I keep looking straight ahead, even though I know a statement like that should be accompanied by a loving gaze towards my spouse, letting Antonia see how much I mean these words. It would be easier to pull off if I *didn't* mean them, but I do. They come from the depths of my soul, and if I look at Layla she will know.

Will hear the truth—and that's against what we agreed upon.

The corner of Antonia's mouth twitches up, a micro-smile. 'Honest answer,' she says, and for the first time since this meeting started I feel a crack in the ice between us.

Luca, unprompted, stands and pads over to the couch, Lego clutched in one fist. He climbs into my lap and buries his face in my shoulder. I wrap an arm around him.

'Ah, good timing. I would like to speak to

him next,' Antonia says, her demeanour changing into something softer. 'May I ask you something, Luca?' she goes on, leaning forward with an open smile.

He peeks out from under my arm, wary but curious.

'You can talk to Antonia,' I say, shifting him around so he's facing her.

'What do you like most about living here?' she asks.

He considers, scrunching his face in thought. 'Layla makes good pancakes,' he says after a beat, and I can feel Layla's laugh vibrate through the air. 'And she teaches me words in Arabic and French. I can say almost all the numbers now. Want to hear?'

Antonia inclines her head. 'I would love that.'

Luca launches into an enthusiastic, if slightly garbled, recitation of the numbers one to ten in French and Arabic. Antonia listens with the patience of a professional, but her features soften even further when he's done. '*Bravo*,' she says, and Luca beams, chest swelling with pride.

I glance at Layla, who's watching me with an expression I can't decipher. My first instinct is to pull away from where our knees touch, to protect myself from the dangerous warmth spreading up my thigh. Instead, I freeze, caught between the urge to lean closer and the voice screaming that this isn't real, that I'm setting myself up for heartbreak when she leaves. I don't move away.

Antonia asks a few more questions, some easy—'What is Luca's favourite activity?'—some thornier—'How will you address questions about his biological parents?' We answer in turns, sometimes overlapping, sometimes pausing to let the other fill the silence. When she asks us how we met, I finally exchange a glance with Layla. The warmth in her eyes I see reflected at me makes my heart stutter.

'We were colleagues first. At the clinic,' she says, and even though this is technically true, the words sound wrong. It glosses over how close we grew as friends before this entire ruse happened. How much she means to me as a person. 'I admired Marina's drive, the way she ran the clinic with so much compassion but also…no nonsense.' She smiles at me, and my pulse picks up pace. 'We started spending more time together outside of work, and eventually realised there was something more.'

I nod along, but the words on my tongue are truer than the script we rehearsed. 'I never thought I'd find someone who cared about the work as much as I did. Or someone who'd take Luca into their heart so completely, given the circumstances. Layla is an amazing person with a big heart and doesn't hesitate to give.'

Layla's smile falters, then returns, but softer now. 'It happened before I even realised it. He's a special kid.'

Antonia closes her notebook, takes off her glasses and sets them on the armrest. The move has the gravitas of a judge preparing to deliver a verdict. 'I have to say, I'm impressed by how united you are,' she says, looking back and forth between us. 'Sometimes these interviews feel like interrogations, but with you two it's clear—' she hesitates, searching for the right word '—that there is real affection here. Even in the small things.'

My lungs seize. I want to grab Layla and hug her, kiss her until her lips are bruised. Not just because she's helping me keep my boy in my home, but for her support outside of it all. For the love she's given him. The time and affection she willingly gave me.

As if reading my thoughts, Layla flips our hands around, linking my fingers with hers. The contact is featherlight, but enough to ground me.

Antonia stands, shuffling her papers into a tidy stack before closing the folder and dropping it into her oversized handbag. 'If I may be honest, I had my reservations at first. The arrangement is...unusual. But after today, I'm confident Luca is lucky to have you both.' She sets down the stack and extends her hand, first to me, then

Layla. Her grip is warm, unhurried. 'There will be some additional paperwork, but you have my recommendation for final approval.'

It takes a second for the words to register. I'm not sure if it's the relief or the crappy sleep from the night before or the sudden possibility of a future not hanging by a thread, but my eyes sting and I have to blink twice to clear my vision.

Layla's grip around my hand tightens with the same energy. Her smile is wide, and when she looks at me there's something in it I can't name, but it burns as bright as the Sicilian sun at noon. It creates just as much heat.

'Thank you,' I say, unable to form any other words. 'Really.'

Antonia offers a small nod and steps out of the door, her sensible shoes barely making a sound as she disappears down the hallway.

For a moment, all three of us just sit there, suspended in the aftershock. Well, Layla and I are in shock. Luca is wriggling in my arms, desperate to get back to his Lego construction site. I set him down on the floor, watching him pad back into his corner.

His corner that will remain his. Because I got the decree of suitability. Luca is mine.

Luca is the first to say something. 'Can I have a snack now?' he asks, voice hopeful.

Layla laughs, the tension melting off her in

waves. 'Absolutely, *habibi*,' she says, and disappears into the kitchen.

I sink back into the couch, every muscle going slack, and let the tears finally spill over. For the first time in months, I feel like I can breathe.

When Layla returns, she hands me a mug of tea and curls up beside me, legs tucked underneath her like she's always belonged here.

'See? We're a model family,' she jokes, but her voice is unsteady.

I don't answer at first, just nestle into her shoulder and close my eyes. For a little while, I let myself believe it's true.

Dinner goes by as usual with Layla and me sharing the kitchen while Luca cheers us on. I keep looking back towards the living room, expecting something to be different. To reflect the change I feel inside me. We have passed the final test; surely the walls know and should show it?

Instead, it's just home. The same as before, and yet something tastes foreign in the air. Changed, but not in the way I expected. Like I'm standing at the edge of a cliff, waiting for the wind to blow me one way or the other.

Luca is giddy from all the adult attention and two helpings of pistachio gelato, so I let him stay up late and read on the living room rug while I flit around the house, tidying to calm my mind.

Layla perches at the kitchen counter, scrolling her phone and occasionally glancing over at us, the line of her jaw soft in the lamplight.

By the time I finish the dishes and coax Luca into pyjamas he's a bundle of post-gelato energy, bouncing on his mattress and reciting Arabic numbers in a singsong voice. I wrangle him into bed with the practised patience of someone who's done this a thousand times and will do it a thousand more. It still amazes me how easy it is now, to love this child—how quickly he slipped under my ribs and made himself essential.

'Mamma?' he asks, pulling the blanket up to his chin.

'Yes, *tesoro*?'

'Are you still going to be my *mamma* tomorrow?'

The question stops me cold. I kneel beside the bed and brush hair off his forehead. 'Of course. Why would you ask?'

He shrugs, a tiny movement. 'Sometimes people go away.'

I swallow. 'I'm not going anywhere, Luca. Not today, not tomorrow.' I kiss his forehead and say it again, softer. 'I promise.'

Luca nods, a strange sense of depth in this gesture that's almost too much for a four-year-old. But he's also seen far more than a child his age should and been through far more in this adoption process. I tried shielding him as much as possible through all of this, but even a small lad like himself is bound to notice all these people asking questions of me, of him.

I'm about to turn on the nightlight when he asks, 'And what about Layla? Is she someone who doesn't go away?'

A lump appears in my throat at the question, and I struggle to swallow it. I know they've bonded, and I enjoyed seeing them grow closer—maybe too much now that he's asking this question. It's been three months since she arrived, and it seems so much longer. So much shorter, too.

But she's a part of the fabric of this family, even though at the beginning we both agreed she shouldn't be. Neither of us has actively pursued this goal, but somehow it has happened anyway.

And I don't know what to say. But I have to say something.

'Layla…' I pause to clear my throat. 'She's a good friend to us both. And friends might go to live somewhere else, but they always remain part of us. Does that make sense to you?'

Luca blinks a few times, fighting off the sleepiness to listen to me. It's the best answer I have right now, and my pulse stuttering tells me I must speak to Layla about this. Because things have changed between us in a way neither of us expected.

We can't ignore it even if the cowardly part inside me—the part that still fears getting too close to someone so intertwined in my life—wants to do just that.

He closes his eyes, accepting it as truth for now, and I wait until his breathing evens out before I turn off the light. As I ease the door shut, I hear the familiar buzz of Layla's phone in the kitchen, the vibration urgent in the quiet house.

Layla answers on the first ring, voice brisk and professional. I linger in the hallway, not eavesdropping exactly, but unable to resist the pull of her half-whispered conversation. She stands with her back to me, one hand braced on the counter, the other pressed tight to her ear.

'Yes, I understand,' she says, pacing a tight circle. 'No, I appreciate the update and offer, really. I need—' Her voice drops, and I can't make out the rest, only the cadence of her steps as she goes into her room.

I'm sitting down on the sofa, heart in my throat, when she exits her room again, looking straight at me. Her expression is inscrutable, which sets me off almost immediately, because it's so unlike her. For as long as I've known her, she's worn her heart on her sleeve.

'What happened?' I ask, because that's the only thing I can think of.

'The New Health Frontier office called. Just now, while you were putting Luca to bed.' Her words turn something to ice within me, and for a second I can't process anything but the way her mouth moves. 'They said Nasser asked them to reopen my case and look into it. They finished their investigation. The old report was full of holes—not just inconsistencies, but actual misstatements. They've lifted the sanctions, effective immediately. And as…compensation, or whatever you want to call it—' She swallows, gaze skating away from mine. 'They're offering me a transfer to one of the field hospitals with open positions. Effective immediately, if I want it.'

My chest goes weirdly light and tight at the same time. The logical part of my brain should be celebrating; this is what we worked for, what she wanted, what I promised I'd help her achieve. But the rest of me is stuck on the phrase 'if I want it'—the way it hovers in the air, turning every centimetre of skin to pins and needles.

I manage to say, 'That's—amazing. Really.' My body won't quite obey. I want to get up, to hug her, do something that makes it real. But I'm glued to the sofa.

Her laugh is short and barely there. 'Yeah, it is. I knew he'd follow through, but I wasn't expecting the apology. Or an immediate transfer offer. It's all happening really fast.'

She looks at me as if she's searching for some sign that I'm angry or hurt. I'm not—I mean, I am, but not at her. And I must keep it together. Layla doesn't owe me anything and what she's done for me… I could try for the rest of my life to put it into words, and I'd still fail. Since I know this is what she wants, I have to find it in me to be glad for her, regardless how it tears my heart apart.

'Where do you want to go?' I ask, and I hate how my voice sounds. Too soft. Needy. The last thing I want her to think is that I want her to stay.

I do, but I can't admit it. It's not right to confront her with that choice.

Layla frowns, and I can see the thought that goes into choosing her next words. 'That's what I've worked for, isn't it? I mean, it's what I wanted. *Want.*' She laughs again, but even Luca would hear the wobble in it. 'I don't have to go right away. There's paperwork, and I'll need to wrap things up here with us and the adoption, but—yeah. That's the offer. I don't think they'd take kindly to me turning it down, not after this whole mess.'

There's a pause, leaving room for the things she's not saying. I can feel it hanging between us, heavy, almost bruising.

'No, of course…' I don't sound as convincing as I want to be, at least not to my ears. All I can hope is that I'm a better actress than I give myself credit for.

Layla, hovering in the doorway until now, walks towards me and takes a seat in the armchair to my left. She perches at the edge, leaving less space between us than she could have. I'm not sure I understand what it means—if it means anything. Maybe I'm making things up.

'The weird thing is… I got exactly what I wanted, but instead of jumping at it, I said I'd think about it.' She looks down at her lap, where her hands are wound into a tight knot. 'I mean, I should be happy, right? It's what I've been pushing for. All those emails, all the calls. But—' She trails off, and when she looks at me there's a flicker of something close to fear. 'I've come to like it here with you. And I know I shouldn't say that because we have an agreement. But… I don't know if I want it any more.'

My heart stopped beating at the first part of her speech and kicks in with double the speed at the end. A part of me doesn't want to believe I'm hearing right, that she could *really* be saying all the things I've wanted her to say. I reach for her hand and she lets me hold it, our fingers interlaced and trembling.

'Then don't go,' I say, before I can talk myself out of it. Can it be this simple? If we both want it…

She smiles wistfully. 'It's not that simple. I can't just stay. There's Luca, there's the clinic, there's you, and I want all of it. But I also want to be out there, in the field. I want to be where it's dangerous and help people there. Just because I found you doesn't mean I've changed—that my desires have changed. You understand, right?'

I do. God, do I ever.

We sit like that for a long time, the clock ticking in the background, counting down to whatever future we'll have to build from the fragments of these moments we've spent together. How we accidentally built a relationship worth preserving in the process of this fake marriage.

'So, what are we going to do about this? I want you to stay, want you to be a part of this family for real. But I understand your need to be elsewhere. I just don't know if I can have someone so impermanent in Luca's life.' I think of what he said to me earlier, my chest squeezing tight. 'He's lost his birth parents already. I want to give him the most stable home possible.'

Even if it means I can't have you.

Layla nods. I see the hurt ripple over her face and the knowledge that I can't do anything to ease it sinks into me. But she nods, because of course she understands. How could she not? She's been so free with her affection and love for Luca—for me—I haven't once doubted she would make whatever choice is best for him.

We sit quietly, chasing our own thoughts. Eventually, she lets go of my hand and moves to get up, pulling me along with her. 'Let's go to bed,' she says. 'We won't figure this out today.'

She pulls me towards my bedroom. The door closes and Layla's mouth finds mine with no hesitation. All my thoughts about the future and impossible choices get knocked clean out of my head. I'm kissing her back hungrily, pulling at her hips—maybe too rough, but she only laughs into my mouth, hands already working under the hem of my shirt. Every inch of me aches for her, even as logic buzzes in the background, begging me not to want this so much.

But I never listen to logic where Layla is concerned.

She's here and tangled up with me, lips on my neck, her breath hot against my skin. There's a high chance I'm blushing from collarbone to hairline, but I barely care. I want to undo all her buttons, learn what her laughter sounds like when she's about to come, relearn every place on her body that makes her shiver.

I fist both hands in her T-shirt, bracing myself.

Maybe to steady my heart against my ribcage. Maybe to keep from floating off the goddamn planet. 'You're going to destroy me,' I mutter, but it comes out as a sigh more than a warning.

'That's the idea.' Layla nips at my throat and actually laughs, like she can't believe she's letting herself do this either after the conversation we've just had.

My shirt is halfway over my head—her hands are underneath, palms warm against my bare skin, the brush of her nails against my nipples enough to make me gasp—when the landline rings with a loud shrill.

For a full second we freeze, tangled, panting. I want to ignore it, let the phone ring itself into silence—but a second later, it registers: the landline only rings for emergencies. My stomach drops through my body, and judging by how Layla pulls my shirt down and takes a step back, she knows it too.

'Dottoressa Moretti? There's a boat—refugees. Dozens, maybe more. Capsized near the port. We need help.'

I confirm the estimated time of arrival of the ambulance and hang up. There's little time to prepare.

Layla stands in the doorway, having listened to my side of the conversation. Her cheeks are still flushed, hair mussed, lips kiss-swollen, and yet she's already shifting back into the alertness of a doctor.

I draw a breath, steadying my voice. 'A refugee boat's gone down near the port. They think dozens of survivors, maybe more. The ambulance is bringing the first wave here.'

Her eyes sharpen. 'We need to prep for hypothermia. Saltwater aspiration. Crush injuries from debris.' She says it flatly, a triage sheet come to life.

'Exactly.' I tug my shirt into place, though it still feels like the heat of her hands lingers on my skin. 'We'll need every blanket we've got, IV fluids ready, oxygen, antibiotics. I'll be right behind you.'

She's already pulling her boots on. 'I'll get everything ready. You'll call Magda to watch Luca?'

Despite the adrenaline spiking through my veins, my chest softens at how natural it is for her to ask about Luca. The first thought after assessing our workload. I nod and as I pick up the phone to call my neighbour, who has watched Luca before in emergencies like this one, I realise I can't let her go.

Yes, our entire relationship is based on a lie. But these feelings are real, and if I keep focusing on the past—on how we are colleagues and how this has come back to haunt me—I might pass up something great.

Something you only find once in life.

Considering the risk, isn't it worth at least a try?

CHAPTER ELEVEN

Layla

BY THE TIME the ambulance screeches into the car park I'm so hyped on adrenaline my teeth ache from clenching. Marina is already on the ramp, hair yanked into a messy bun, latex gloves snapped tight, as the paramedics wrestle the back doors open. Blue strobe splashes over everything: the pitted walls, the creaking trolley, even the plastic ponchos thrown over the triage team.

The first patient is a woman, maybe twenty, so soaked that her baggy trousers stick to her calves like skin. She has the ghost-lips of advanced hypothermia—edges blued so deep I'm worried necrosis is already happening. Her left arm is curled and bent in a way that makes me look twice; there's a clean puncture above the elbow, and I can see bone where the skin is sticking out.

I don't wince—years of experience have beaten that impulse out of me—but I know she must be in a lot of pain. Her eyes are glazed over, each breath drawing in as a raspy struggle. With such a break, I'm surprised she's not…

'Marina, I think she might be going into shock,' I say, my gaze slipping from the woman's blue lips to the film of sweat clinging to her, mingling with the ocean water.

Marina takes one look and yells, 'Room two—now!' Her voice snaps the paramedics into action. We wheel the woman through the double doors, tyres rattling over the cracked tiles. Marina is already at her side, one hand bracing the IV pole, the other on the stethoscope she's pressing hard against the woman's chest.

'She's got a thready radial, but she's conscious,' she says as I cut away the remains of her jacket with trauma shears.

'She won't be for long,' I reply, working on getting access to the woman while Marina connects the monitor. She's already got the pulse ox clipped to a raw finger, and I frown at the number. 'O2 sats are bad, thirty-four C and dropping. We need warm fluids, stat. Let's get blankets in here as well, pile them high.'

I reach for the IV kit, hands stiff with cold. The woman's vein is collapsed from dehydration or shock—could be both. I blow out a breath, try to find the thread of calm I had an hour ago, and go in at a shallow angle. The flashback's weak, but I get it, and start the drip.

The old clinic monitors flicker to life with a whine, sticky pads plastered to blue-white skin. Heart rate's in the fifties. Respiration slow, shallow, and she keeps trying to roll off the trolley like she's got somewhere better to be.

Marina pins the good shoulder, makes eye contact with me. 'She's not responding to the thermal pads. We might have to go invasive.'

My mind ticks through the steps—central line, lavage, intubation if it gets any worse. But before I can even ask, Marina's already prepping the femoral, voice like steel. I loop the oxygen over the woman's face then rush to the supply closet to grab the blankets and warm water bottles we prepped as we waited for the ambulance to arrive.

'Give me the trauma shears,' Marina says. I toss them, and she slices the rest of the woman's sweater off. Underneath, the skin is marbled with bruises and debris gashes from whatever shrapnel was in the water. Salt has already crusted over the wounds.

I start to flush one of the deeper cuts and blood wells up, bright against the blue skin.

Marina doesn't say anything, just adjusts the mask over the woman's nose and starts to splint the broken arm. The limb is a dead weight, no reflex, and her lips flatten as she sets the bones. 'On my count,' she tells me, and I know to hold the shoulder and anchor the elbow.

'One, two—' Marina braces, pulls and sets. There's a sickening pop and the woman musters a cry even in her state, but the alignment is better and when Marina wraps the makeshift splint it holds.

'She's lost a lot of blood,' I murmur, trying to free up a hand to start a pressure bandage. But Marina's already two steps ahead, pressing gauze into my palm and taping the edges.

The synergy is incredible, the kind of thing you see on TV where everyone works together seamlessly. But this is real and it's happening, and I can't tell if I'm in awe of Marina or about to cry from relief that we haven't lost anyone yet. The night is still young and the paramedics keep triaging by the port.

When the woman's heart rate starts to edge up—sixty, then seventy—and her breaths deepen, I finally let myself exhale. The monitors are ancient, but the data holds: she's stabilising.

I reach up to wipe sweat off my face and realise it's not sweat, it's saltwater. Or tears, maybe. Not the sad kind but maybe relief. I might not be in the field, but this woman needed someone today and I was here. I helped, and I will continue to help until it's time to leave.

Which apparently is sooner than I thought. The call from Nasser's office caught me completely off-guard, and only as we're slowing down here do I let the thoughts come back.

They reversed the decision, removed the mark on my file, and as a gesture of goodwill they're transferring me to the next available assignment. I'm free to leave Sicily much sooner than I thought—getting exactly what I wanted.

If it's still what I want. But it's not. Except it is.

This is the loop I get stuck in when I let myself think about it too hard. I push it away again, focusing on the situation in front of us. In the distance, I can already hear the wailing of an ambulance. There will be more patients soon.

Marina leans in, checks the woman's pupils, then stands back. 'That'll hold for now,' she says, voice softer. The hard edge is gone, replaced by the flat fatigue of someone running on empty and knowing there's more to come.

The next patient is already en route. The crisis will roll on, but for one second we stand together, breathing the same over-warm air, hands sticky and tired and shaking, and I wonder how I ever managed to work without her.

Then the doors crash open again and we're moving, hearts synced, brains back in the game, already halfway to the next table before the trolley's stopped moving.

Countless hours later we're past the worst of it, but the clinic is still jittering on the fumes of adrenaline. The outer corridor hums with the chorus of the newly triaged—coughs, tears, the occasional fight breaking out in dialects I barely understand—but back here, in the makeshift office, I take a break.

None of the patients left here are critical. Some will stay here, with Marina and I each taking a shift. But right now, we're waiting for a few people to get evacuated to the nearest hospital. The helicopter has already landed once and we're expecting a few more flights.

When the paramedics delivered the last of the people, they hung back to help, telling us that the boat got caught in a huge storm. They'd barely made it to shore. That explained the degree of injuries we've seen today.

I'm half-folded against a stack of gauze rolls, my scrubs stuck to my back with dried sweat and my knees from repeated bouts with the wet floor. My stethoscope dangles from my hand; I don't remember when I started squeezing it so tight the bell leaves a permanent dent in my palm.

Marina's across from me, perched on a sterilisation crate, one leg bent, bandaging her own hand, rubbed raw on the latex glove. Her fingers tremble as she cinches the gauze, blood already seeping through the pad. There are dark rings under her eyes and dried sweat crystallising at her hairline. If that is how she looks, I must look even worse.

For a long time, neither of us speaks. We don't

need to. The silence is loaded as we come down from the whirlwind of the evening. My eyes dart to the clock hanging on the wall—I haven't checked the time throughout this entire incident.

Four in the morning. Holy heck.

'Luca needs to be ready for his playgroup in three hours,' I say automatically.

Marina lifts her head, looking at me for some quiet seconds. Then she bursts out laughing. The sound rumbles through the air, catching me off-guard, but within a second I'm joining her until we're both bent over, laughing, because the alternative is to burst into tears from exhaustion.

'I love that your first thought is about Luca. It's strange, I didn't realise how lonely I'd grown since starting the adoption journey with him—since Agron passed. But I love how I'm not the only person thinking about this now,' Marina says, her expression growing softer with each word. 'I think I'm in love with you, Layla.'

My body runs hot and cold all at once, my pulse thudding so loud I can hear it in my ears. Feel it at the back of my throat. The answering call in my chest is as unexpected as it is clear: what I feel for her goes beyond casual. My affection for her has crept up on me, slipping in through the cracks as we went on this adventure together to save Luca from being deported.

I agreed to it because I could never sit by and

let this family be torn apart. But I've since become a part of them, and they of me. Like the escalation of our attraction has just been the precursor for my growing feelings, which have kept themselves hidden away. Until now.

'Marina…' I push myself straight, ignoring the ache in my muscles as I step closer until I'm within her reach. 'I'm in love with you, too.'

She wraps her arms around my waist, eliminating the final few centimetres of space left between us. We're both sticky with sweat and seawater, but in this moment I don't care. Not when my heart is both soaring from the truth and tenderness of this moment while also already cracking in half. Because confessions aside, I know what's about to happen next.

It's a thought that's been coming back to me over and over as we jumped from one crisis to the next. And I've never been so devastated to have my mind made up.

'You're not staying, are you?' Marina asks, and of course she already knows. It's as if my attempts to stay clear of her—to not catch any feelings—have been a wasted effort from the very start.

I shake my head because my throat is suddenly too tight to say anything. Pressure builds behind my eyes, and I blink a few times to disperse it, but it just keeps on coming.

'I can't,' I say after a few silent moments. 'A

part of me wants to because I love you and Luca, and these last few months have been nothing like I could have imagined.'

Marina presses her face against my stomach, and I wind my fingers through her hair, loosening the already dishevelled bun sitting at her nape. A zing of electricity runs through me as I touch her—and she me—and there's a small voice in my brain yelling at me to not be stupid. To take this version of life, even if it's nothing like I imagined it would be. Even if I fear losing an important piece of myself in the process. How important can it be if I must give her—*them*—up for it?

'But your heart wants to be out there and living the life you worked so hard to achieve. The one you almost lost because of your backstabbing supervisor.' Marina says it without bitterness, and somehow her understanding is even more devastating than if she'd cursed me for this decision.

'I just—' I pause, unable to find the right words to say. Or maybe I don't know if I should say anything at all.

'You don't owe me an explanation,' Marina mumbles as if reading my mind. And it's because of that knowledge, the certainty that she accepts me the way I am, that I *want* to grant her a glimpse. I want to express the things I never have before.

'My mum used to be career-minded. Not a doctor, but the first woman in her family to get a higher education—to make plans for the future. And I know what they say: *God laughs at our plans*, right? It was true for her. She met my dad, fell pregnant with me and then that became her life.'

My mother has always been the driving force behind my ambition. Of course, my father was there too, wanting to see excellence. But he would have been happy with me landing some comfortable stop in a family practice in Algiers. It's Mum's influence that pushed me towards New Health Frontier and applying my skills to the people most in need. It's her I'm thinking about now as my chest becomes so tight it's impossible to breathe.

'She wanted more in life, and she never got to have it. Growing up in a family which didn't place a lot of value on her independence, she had to struggle to get where she wanted to be. And she gave it all up because of me. Settling down feels like I'm making a mistake she showed me to avoid through her life experience.'

I squeeze my eyes shut, sucking in a breath that is eighty percent salt, twenty percent uncertainty. My throat feels scraped raw, but I keep going.

'She wanted a life outside the house, outside her prescribed story. And she didn't get it. I owe it to her and… I guess, to myself. Or maybe I'm scared that if I don't go, I'll just—' I fumble for the words. 'I'll disappear.'

It comes out all tangled and clumsy, but Marina listens. She listens the way nobody ever has, eyes steady and dark and aching with something I can barely let myself acknowledge. She presses her cheek into my stomach, wraps her arms tight around my hips and says nothing for long enough that my pulse steadies. Just a little.

'Anything I could tell you right now about a mother's instincts you probably already heard. Have probably already told yourself. It's not my place to convince you otherwise.' This answer is so *her*, and it should fill me with the confidence that I've made the right decision. But it has the opposite effect. Makes me waver because I've never been on clear footing anyway. Not with her.

'Does it have to mean the end for us?' I ask, hating how much my voice strains against the words—almost swallowing instead of letting them out. Scared to know the answer.

I feel her chest expand, pressing against my body in a way that feels far too familiar for what is about to happen to us. The sigh she lets out penetrates my scrub top and heats my skin. Or maybe it's the anticipation that's causing the temperature to rise. How have I not seen this coming when this entire thing was designed to be impermanent?

Even hoping seems foolish now.

'I have to think about what's right for Luca. His life is only now starting to come into a more permanent shape. After losing his dad and all the stress the adoption process put him through—I can't add another uncertainty to his life.'

The words land like cold stones in my stomach, sinking until the pressure is almost enough to cave my ribs in. A memory comes up unbidden: Luca curled on the couch, his back pressed into mine as he whispers his way from one to ten in French again and again, like a secret mantra. She's right to protect him. This is his home. It could be mine too, if I let it. But what if I don't know how to stay put? What if I'm just built to leave? Maybe I'll never know unless I actually try.

I blink against the burn behind my eyes, fighting to get my thoughts in order. 'I get that,' I say, even though my voice cracks on the last word. I shouldn't keep pressing, but apparently I'm programmed for agony. 'But you know I'd never just disappear. I'd stay in touch if you let me.' A hollow promise, but better than nothing. 'If that helps.'

'I know,' Marina says quietly, finally pushing herself upright so our faces are nearly level. She looks the way I feel—bleary-eyed, hollowed out by too many hours and too much feeling, but stubbornly alive. 'I don't want you to leave and for us to become strangers. I want to hear how you're doing and where your adventures take you. But…'

Not as we are now, She's too kind to say it. And the truly heartbreaking part is that I understand. It's why the fight leaves my body even before I can muster the words. She's right, of course. Luca is her utmost priority, and I would never ask her to choose otherwise.

'I get it. Wrong place, wrong time—isn't that what they say?' *They* being a very vague term, and I've hit the right tone because Marina's mouth twitches with a wry smile.

'We still have some time left to enjoy this, if you want. Until your transfer comes through. But I also understand if you'd rather make a clean break now. Rip off the plaster.' There's a hesitation in her voice that's unlike Marina. She's worried…about rejection?

I lift my hands to her face, pulling her closer and sliding my mouth over hers. It's a tender kiss, filled with my longing for this woman. I could spend the rest of my life kissing her like that and I know I'd never get tired of it. But could I spend the rest of my life here on Sicily, raising her beautiful boy with her, when I feel my heart call to whatever is out there as much as it does to her?

'You're a doctor. You should know that ripping off plasters isn't advisable. You might rip the wound open,' I say, desperately needing some lightness after the night we've had. But also, even if I thought it would be easier to let her go now, I know it won't. Not while I live in her house and see her every day.

We'll have to make the best of whatever time we have left. There are many things to discuss—the logistics of wrapping up the adoption, staying married on paper for the time being until things are sorted and we can split without causing any suspicion. We've outlined it all in the agreement we first signed, so it's a matter of following our own blueprint.

But right now, I don't want to think about any of it. I just want to be.

CHAPTER TWELVE

Layla

It's been far too long since I last did this: stand in the dusty stairwell of an Algiers apartment block, count the heavy, scuffed tiles as I ascend, and rehearse the script of normal daughterhood. On every landing, old cigarette smoke and the scent of bleach fight to the death. By the time I'm on the fourth floor, my tongue feels thick and foreign in my mouth.

There's a doormat at the threshold, faded to the colour of sand. I don't bother knocking. My mother expects me to open the door myself. I let her know I'd be stopping by at home for a few days before catching the flight New Health Frontier has organised for me to get to my next post.

The news about my transfer reached me two weeks after the fateful conversation Marina and I had about our future together. A boulder has been sitting in the pit of my stomach ever since that night, and I was sure it would dissolve once

I turned my back on Sicily—*not* on Marina or Luca, who I still speak to daily.

Turns out I was wrong. Each kilometre I travel only seems to increase the weight.

I push the door open, calling out a greeting as I take off my shoes and pull my luggage out of the way. Inside, it's dark and humid, the kind of atmosphere I associate with end-of-summer blackouts. The faint rambling of a television drifts down the corridor.

'Layla!' my mother calls from the kitchen, and it's odd to finally hear her voice in person and not over the phone. 'Don't forget your shoes, please. The floor has just been cleaned.'

I stare down at my bare feet, smiling. No matter how many years I stay away, I will never forget the most fundamental rule in my mother's place: no shoes allowed.

'Your flight was okay?' she asks, back still turned, arm already elbow-deep in a basin of mint leaves. The smell permeates the air and it's such a familiar sight—and taste—the way my heart squeezes inside my chest takes me by surprise. Longing wells up inside me, but not for this place. It's not about being back home.

It's what *home* has come to represent. It *should* be this place I'm thinking of, with the smell of my mother's cooking lingering beneath the strong scent of mint.

I walk over to the sink, kissing my mother's cheek, and she tuts at me affectionately, not minding the interruption as much as she pretends.

'Delayed an hour. French air traffic control striking again and delaying all of Europe,' I say, and it's so easy, this exchange of gripes. It doesn't matter how long I've been gone—we slip right into the rhythm. It's almost enough to distract me from the things brewing within me. 'Where do you want my bag?'

'In your old bedroom. Don't mind the sheets—I forgot to iron.'

I lug my huge suitcase through the too-small apartment, grazing my elbow on the sharp corner of the wall. My mother's rules are still clear as day in my head, but apparently I forgot the proportions of the walls, feeling almost awkward. I count the old signs of domesticity—the photo wall with me at various stages of my life, the incense burners arrayed on the bookshelf, the sewing machine doubling as a plant stand whenever my mother isn't using it. My old room doubles as a storage space now, with an exercise bike gathering dust in one corner. I drop the bag onto the bed, hesitating for a moment.

The sense of overwhelm that started ever since I got the transfer news has only grown over the flight. Now that I'm back in my old home, I thought it would leave. Even though my room has changed, the reminders of my old life are still here. Like the stack of books my mother used to read me during bedtime. They were children's books, sure. But as I scan the titles, it becomes clear they were carefully picked to show me the path she hasn't walked. They all feature female characters going on adventures, or learning things, or saving the world.

Yet all I can think about is how much I want to turn around and forget about everything. Build a nest with the woman I love and who loves me. I still don't know how to hold these two things in my heart at the same time.

I return to the kitchen before those thoughts can overwhelm me. Spending some time with my mother is the right call. She'll remind me of that piece inside me I'm scared to lose. She's the one who inspired it in the first place—grew me into the person who wants more for herself.

She's already got the tea on the stove. When I walk in, she doesn't look at me as she says, 'Sit, *habibti*. I will pour.'

I obey and let my gaze drift around the kitchen. The cracked tile floor, patched with duct tape at the places the grout has surrendered. That looks like my father's shoddy craftsmanship. He's no doubt lecturing interns on proper bedside manner while our kitchen floor caves in.

My mother pours tea from a battered pot once

belonging to my grandmother into two tiny glasses. She holds both in one hand, brings them to the table and sets one exactly at my right. She then slides into the seat across from me and levels her gaze on me.

'You look thin,' she says first thing.

I open my mouth to protest, but she's already moved on, her own glass clinking lightly against the saucer. 'Did you eat on the plane?'

'They gave us bread and cheese. I'm not starving.'

'You'll eat soon,' she says. 'I made *mhajeb*.'

The leftover ache in my chest does a weird lurch at this. My mother's *mhajeb* is legendary, the kind of food that lures expat children home from any distance, international or existential. It's almost enough to make me believe for a moment that the world is simple, that my choices don't sprawl messily in every direction.

'You didn't have to—' I start, but she waves me off.

'If my daughter is coming home, I make *mhajeb*. What else is a mother for?'

I smile, though the question—*what else is a mother for?*—finds its way inside my already fortified chest. Or at least I thought I had steeled myself on the flight back here, determined to let the fake stuff with Marina be gone and hang onto the friendship we formed. The bond I have with Luca.

I have no business thinking of him when I hear the word *mother*. That's not who I am to him, no matter how many nights I've put him to bed or how often I've cooked him breakfast.

Why did I never make *mhajeb* for him? The thought hurts, barrelling through me without warning, and I blink the familiar pressure behind my eyes away. Mum will have questions and there's no way I can explain it to her.

As if picking up on my thoughts, Mum studies me with that look—the one that can read every unsaid word.

'You said you're starting your new assignment? Is it in the Congo again?' Mum tears off small pieces of the *mhajeb* with her fingers, blowing on them before popping them into her mouth, chewing slowly as she waits for my answer.

'No, I'm not going back to the Democratic Republic of Congo. After how things shook out with my old supervisor, I didn't want to go back there.' Not that New Health Frontier had offered it. Their list had omitted the DRC and we all know why. 'I'm heading to South Sudan this time, back into the field.'

Mum's brow knits together. 'And that's better than the post in Sicily?'

I pause, not having anticipated the question. Or how there wouldn't be an immediate, resounding, *Yes. Of course, it's better. I want to be in South*

Sudan and not in Sicily. What's so hard to understand about that?

Why do you have to convince yourself so hard of the truth, Layla?

'It's what I want to do. I know Dad would be happier if I went into a family practice, but it seems a waste when I can do so much good in places like South Sudan.' We're retreading old ground here, but at least my mother's been supportive of my ambitions.

'Oh, was the clinic in Sicily a family practice?' Mum asks with a genuine look of confusion on her face.

'What? No, it's a clinic run with the help of New Health Frontier.' That's a gross oversimplification of the tremendous work Marina does mostly on her own, but if I start to talk about her, I will definitely lose the paper-thin composure I'm holding onto.

'I see.' Mum picks up her cup, blowing on it despite the tea already being cold, and stares at me over the rim. 'Why change then? Sounded like you started to enjoy yourself there, last time we spoke.'

I rock back in my chair, hands curled tight around the sweating glass of tea, and stare at the wall behind my mother's head like the splatter of magnets and thumbtacks there is going to give me an answer. The question isn't that hard, but suddenly my head is a blender—everything in it swirling so fast none of it actually makes sense once I reach for it.

Why change?

Shouldn't this answer be second nature by now? Shouldn't I be rattling off stories about the boat crisis, the all-nighters, the countless times I got to actually save someone's life in Sicily? And how it hasn't been fulfilling me as much as the field hospital has—and will?

But all I can think of are the weeks I spent working with Marina, growing roots and pretending not to notice them until overnight I was wrapped in them. Or how I know I actually made a difference, how I didn't waste my degree by going down this path of selfless service.

But I don't say any of those things. I hesitate, which is almost worse. It creates a space where before I was clinging onto the certainty that this *is* what I wanted. A tiny opening that whispers, *Is it really what you want?*

My mother keeps watching me, picking at the *mhajeb* on her plate.

'It's not that I didn't enjoy it,' I finally say, pushing past the weird lump in my throat. 'I did. The work was good there.'

I can't lie to my mother, even though I know I should, because being honest is about to open the box I've kept buried inside me since I left

Sicily behind. Or maybe even since Nasser's office called me.

But why do I feel the need to keep it buried?

Mum's eyebrow raises slightly, the perfect arch, as intimidating now as it was when I was growing up. 'You met someone.'

Her certainty catches me off-guard, the cup with my cold tea freezing halfway to my face. And it's the hesitation before I can muster a denial that tells her she's guessed right. So I swallow it down, and instead say, 'How did you know?'

My mother snorts into her tea. 'Don't act surprised. You have the same look now you had the day I caught you with that girl in your bedroom and you tried to tell me she was here to study chemistry.' She points a perfectly manicured finger at my chest like that will pin the memory to me. 'Layla, whenever you think you're hiding something, it turns into a neon sign above your head.'

Heat flushes instantly up my neck, way outpacing the logic circuits trying to offer a response. 'That was…years ago,' I say, but my voice cracks halfway through.

Mum just looks victorious, folding a new piece of *mhajeb* with exaggerated care. 'You turned red then, too. I thought you'd faint from panic the way you tried to insist girls don't even kiss each other—"scientific impossibility, Mum".'

'I'm not hiding anyone in my room this time,' I reply. 'And it's not like this was something serious. We just connected for a while, but we both agreed from the start it wouldn't be anything.'

'Why not?'

Because, Mother, this was a fake marriage for us to kind of commit adoption fraud. And yeah, I've fallen in love with my fake wife and her real kid, but that doesn't change anything between us.

'Because… I always knew I was going to leave, and she has a child, so she needs someone permanent in her life.'

Mum's lips disappear into a thin line, and I can tell she's not buying it. Which is a problem since I'm telling the truth. Right? Oh God, why am I not sure?

'You're not making any sense. You said you enjoyed the work you did in Sicily, *and* you also found someone dear to you. Why would you rather be in South Sudan, all by yourself, doing work you said you find as fulfilling as what you were doing in Sicily?'

'No, you don't understand,' I blurt, because honestly, this entire conversation is making my head spin. 'It's not that simple.'

Mum narrows her eyes, but she doesn't interrupt, which is basically an invitation to dig my own grave. So I keep going—because apparently I left my impulse control at the airport.

'Look, Marina is…' I pause, searching for words that don't sound like a tragic song lyric. There aren't any. 'She's incredible, Mum. She's all-in—like, parenting and running this clinic, she's literally building a life for Luca from scratch. And I'm proud of her. But I can't settle down just yet. I've only started my career and what if—what if there is more out there, and I'm being stupid to give it up? I mean, you understand, right?'

I look at her with wide, pleading eyes, but she returns a puzzled look that sends my stomach careening through my body.

She asks, 'Why do you think I should understand, of all people?'

Heard by an outsider, I'm sure they'd think there is a bite to her words, but I can hear the concern underpinning the matter-of-fact question. I've never known her to mince her words or hold back.

I take a deep breath. We've never actually talked about the sacrifices I've seen her make, but I guess now is a good time since I'm already falling apart anyway. Might as well add something on top.

'I know how much you gave up having me. To make sure I could do all this—get through med school, get out of Algeria, actually do something important. You could've done anything, but you were home because of me. I want to honour that sacrifice, and it feels like the only way to do it right is to go all-in on my career. If I stay in one place, if I slow down, isn't that just—' I flounder, gesturing helplessly at the air '—repeating the pattern? Isn't that exactly what you warned me about by pushing me to get educated and have a career?'

I don't know what reaction I was expecting from her, but I know the way her jaw softens isn't it. She looks almost…surprised?

'You think if you put down roots, you'll get trapped. Because you saw it happen to me?'

'That's…yeah. Kind of? I mean, not that your life was a trap,' I add quickly, heat crawling up my neck. 'But you deserved more, and you didn't get it. I shouldn't turn my back on all the things you pushed me towards just because…' I almost say *just because I love someone*, but I bite it back so fast I nearly choke on it.

Mum sets down her tea with a soft clink, eyebrows raised, gaze pinning me like a single spotlight in an interrogation room. 'So, what you're saying is, even though you care about this woman, you're running to South Sudan because you think that's the only way to justify your mother's life?'

I open my mouth. Shut it. Open it again. 'No, this… I don't mean to. *Maman.*'

She raises her hand, shutting me up. 'I'm sure

this is how you've seen it, and there's some truth to it. I did have plans and those got sidelined by your father. And by you, to some extent. But all of these things were my choice. Were there times I wondered what life would be like on the path I didn't take? Of course, but those visions have never been powerful enough to make me regret what I chose.' Mum pauses, shaking her head. 'So you don't have to honour anything because the idea you have is wrong.'

Warmth spreads through me when she reaches over the table to put her hand on top of mine. 'If you want to choose your career, do so. You have my full support. But don't choose it just because I didn't choose mine. I just ask you to think wisely—success will not love you back.'

Later, in the room that used to be mine, I lie on the narrow bed and stare at the ceiling, at the brown water stains that map a topography of old leaks and older summers. I listen to the ticking of the fan, the sound of my mother talking on the phone in the next room, the hiss of traffic and the occasional horn from the street below.

I think of Marina, and Luca, and the way Sicily felt on my skin—like a place I could belong to, even as I was preparing to leave it. I think of all the places I've been, and all the places I haven't, and whether I'll ever stop wanting to go.

In the dark, my mother's words come back to me: *success will not love you back.*

I roll over, tuck my knees to my chest and watch the slow spin of the ceiling fan. I tell myself it's not true, that I'm not running. But I know the truth when I hear it, especially in my mother's voice.

I wonder, not for the first time, if I'll ever figure out what I'm actually running towards.

CHAPTER THIRTEEN

Marina

IT'S ODD TO see the Sunday market lose its splendour like that. Of course, I know nothing has changed about the local farmer's market and whatever I'm feeling is in my head. Has been in my head for several weeks now, ever since…well, truth be told, ever since Luca and I dropped off Layla at the airport.

A part of me wanted to go by myself, keep that final moment in a selfish gesture, but she's become as much a part of his life as mine. I thought he would be more confused—or maybe devastated?—than he was and continues to be. With his father's death and so many strange people coming to talk to him over the last few months, I'm surprised his reaction hasn't been bigger.

Maybe it has something to do with Layla calling from the taxi on her way to her parents' home in Algiers. Or how she calls without fail every night, even if it's just for five minutes to hear about my day and tell me about hers. She doesn't always catch Luca awake, but then we still chat, sometimes for hours, and if I close my eyes as I listen to her talk, I can almost feel her warmth drifting towards me as if she was really there.

'Are you going to buy these tomatoes or just stare at them?' The familiar voice pulls me out of my thoughts, and I whirl around, the vegetable—fruit?—forgotten in my hand.

'Giuseppe, what are you doing here?' It's rare to see him in Pozzallo; seeing as the town is so small, it doesn't really need more than one lawyer. Most of our dealings we've done through phone calls and frantic late-night emails whenever I got the time to look at my inbox.

'Visiting my *mamma*, of course. She sent me out with her weekly shopping list and you're currently holding the tomatoes hostage,' he says, pointedly looking down at my hands.

'Oh…' I hand him the tomatoes I'm holding then step away so he can haggle about the price, mostly because he enjoys it rather than wanting to get the produce for the least amount of money.

Next to me, Luca pulls free from my grip to hug Giuseppe's leg. He's never met a person he didn't instantly become friends with. My heart swells in my chest despite the space there feeling much more constrained than usual.

'*Ehi, Luca, come va?*' Giuseppe tousles Luca's

hair, nodding as my son launches into a long-winded retelling of his day, including many narrative detours. We fall into step next to each other and by the time Luca is done, we're in the cheese section of the market.

'So, where is your lovely wife? I was hoping to meet the mystery woman,' Giuseppe says, and I know what he's not saying—how he thinks I'm full of crap with this marriage. Which I am, but I'm not about to implicate him in this. Friend or not, he's still the lawyer involved in my adoption case and there are ethics rules.

'She left some weeks ago for South Sudan. You know her work takes her into different field hospitals across the globe,' I reply, the answer feeling practised. Before she left, Layla and I agreed we would stay married not just on paper but in front of any relevant people—like Giuseppe and New Health Frontier—and give it at least a year before we decide on anything else. It's not like either of us is involved with anyone else.

He raises an eyebrow. 'Gone already? That didn't take long. We only received the official papers from Albania last month.'

I remember the moment well. Layla and I opened the thick envelope together, falling into each other's arms laughing and crying when the final confirmation came that Luca would stay here with me—with us.

With…me.

Because there is no *us*.

And I know that's what Giuseppe is not so subtly hinting at. I just don't understand why. Does he want me to slip up and admit something he might potentially have to report?

I pluck a chunk of pecorino from the vendor's sample tray, the cheese a salty punch on my tongue, and try not to sound as hollow as I feel. 'Layla's work keeps her moving.' I pause, and then I don't know what possesses me to get so close to the truth, but I do, because the last weeks have been so tiring and I've been all on my own. 'It's tough and I don't know if we made the right decision. Maybe acting fast didn't do us any favours in the relationship.'

Though if I hadn't needed a signed marriage certificate, we likely would have never got as close as we did. She would have moved on to a different assignment, floating out of my life like the countless other people coming to work at the clinic.

We move on and when we come to a stop in front of a café, Giuseppe inclines his head towards the door. 'You sound down. Want to have a coffee and talk about it?'

I shouldn't. With all the things Layla and I pulled, I'd be foolish to sit down with him even though he is my friend. But the loneliness is far more crushing than it's ever been and it's only now I'm realising what the pressure inside my chest is. The lure of someone seeing me—offering to talk—is exactly what I need. So I say yes and walk after Giuseppe as he enters the café.

The inside is slightly too warm, and the little table Giuseppe picks is right beside the kids' play corner. I don't even need to ask Luca if he wants to go check it out; he's across the tiled floor and elbow-deep in a crate of mismatched building blocks before I can shed my coat. Out of habit, my gaze tracks him as he plonks down next to a girl already lining up plastic animals in a neat, obsessive row.

I slide into the chair across from Giuseppe, fighting the urge to fidget. There's a little sugar packet at my place and I press it flat between my thumb and finger, rolling it over and over, like maybe if I do it enough times the sticky ache in my chest will dissolve.

He orders for us, chatting with the barista in that effortless way only a Sicilian native can, then leans back, glasses sliding down the bridge of his nose as he fixes his lawyer-lie-detector stare on me.

'So.' He says it like a challenge. 'What's this about you and your wife not lasting until the end of summer?'

I bristle, though, as it happens, I can admit the

absurdity. It's not like he's wrong. As far as relationships are concerned, ours doesn't appear to be a solid one. But it could have been…if it hadn't been fake. Or is this what I tell myself?

'You know we rushed into this because of circumstances. I've never made a secret about that,' I say, hedging while letting some of my true feelings slip out. *Letting* being quite a generous way to describe it when they actually press against me, making it impossible to swallow them back down. 'We fell for each other, and I was in a bind, so I asked her. We thought it would work. Turns out it's more difficult than meaning well.'

'You thought it would work. But now you don't? Why?' Giuseppe cocks his head, hands folded over his stomach. His words have an interrogative lilt to them, but I know he simply wants to find out how his friend is doing.

'Layla wasn't ever going to stick around. She wants to do fieldwork—the adrenaline, a life of seeing the world while doing good. Meanwhile, I have my life here and with Luca…' I trail off, because I don't know how to explain how I feel now without revealing the true nature of our relationship. 'I thought we would make it work like this—her following her passion and me staying here. I welcomed it because at least it would remove the odd dynamic of me being her supervisor and her wife. After—'

Giuseppe interrupts me with a snort, waving his empty espresso cup in front of him. 'Oh, don't give me that, Marina. I know what happened in Milan, and I'm not minimising any of it. But surely you don't mean to tell me you were worried about the power dynamics if she stayed but now that she's working somewhere else, you also don't like it?'

He has me there, and the precision of his aim almost cracks the facade I've put across this entire Layla situation. I brace my arms on the table, staring at the pale oblong saucer on the table. My mind is a tangle and the thread of logic somewhere in that mess almost invisible. No, we didn't go through all of this for nothing. There are good reasons. Luca…

'I changed my mind,' I say, and in a warped sense it's true. I *need* it to be true. 'The power dynamics would have been a problem, but as she geared up to leave, I realised how bad it would be for Luca to have another adult disappear out of his life. And that's what Layla will do. Come and leave as her career takes her places. I need to keep what's best for him in mind.'

Giuseppe leans forward, a stark line appearing between his brows. 'Wait, you're telling me when she left she just vanished? Not a word to you or Luca?'

'What? No, of course not. She calls him every

day. She calls at bedtime whenever she can, even if it's the middle of the night for her. She's the one who taught him how to say goodnight in six different languages. He's obsessed with impressing her on the phone now.'

'Then what's your excuse, Marina?' He says my name soft and low, and something inside me goes taut at his tone. 'If she still calls every night, and if you clearly miss her, why aren't you trying harder? Giving up without trying doesn't sound like you.'

I want to ignore his words because my mind is made up. It's the right thing to do. Both for me and for her. I need stability and she doesn't want to stop here. And I'd rather feel like this for the rest of my life than be the person forcing her to stop.

It's the right thing to do. It *is*.

Giuseppe tilts his head towards the play area and I follow his gaze, looking at a bright Luca as he exchanges building blocks with another child. It's been an easy change for him to navigate. Almost like nothing has changed at all. If she can't call us, she sends a video message for me to play to him at night before he falls asleep. It's an easy routine we settled into, as familiar and seamless as what we used to have in person.

Luca is happy. Has remained so over the course

of this transition. No, if anyone is beset by clouds and unable to pull themselves out of it, it's me. My inability to… What? I don't even know, and this conversation with Giuseppe is sending my brain into a tailspin. Is he right? Am I feeding him excuses?

Am I swallowing them myself?

'It's not…' I stop because I don't know where the words will lead me. I try for another reason, something explanatory or at least self-effacing, but it comes out soft and miserable: 'I don't know how to do this, Pepe.'

He doesn't interrupt, doesn't offer me platitudes. He just waits, all the little micro-signals of a man who knows I need to talk my way into the truth.

'When Layla was here,' I say, 'it was easy. Maybe too easy. Someone to hand the soap when I ran out washing up, someone who understood the exact amount of time to scramble eggs so Luca wouldn't complain. An extra pair of hands, and intuition, and—' I lose the thread, but he lets me fumble around in my own feelings. 'When she was here, I could just…show her. That I cared. But what we have *does* scare me. Things that feel good tend to disappear from my life. Or morph into something unrecognisable. Maybe the desperation of Luca's situation made everything feel more intense. But… I— Maybe I can't do it from afar.'

He gives a little 'mm' sound, encouragement or agreement. 'So now you're telling me it's easier to never try at all? Because you have never been at a distance. Never been forced to adapt.'

I hate how right he is. The idea of loving someone at a distance and letting it hang unrequited terrifies me. I'd rather kill it off at the root, suffocate it with reality, than leave it exposed to the whiplash and burn of longing. Of the uncertainty that comes with what Layla wants against what I need to feel safe.

'I think I hoped she'd stay here,' I say. It's humiliating, even now. 'Not forever, just longer than this. And when she said she couldn't, it was…easier to close the book rather than read the pages out of order.' I press my thumb so hard into the sugar packet the grains threaten to burst from the seam. Getting so close to the truth of my feelings makes the words spill out unfiltered.

'I get Francesca has made you cautious, but this seems on the extreme side when I know you hit it off and have feelings for each other.' He pauses, clearing his throat, and his gaze grows sharper. 'The relationship might have started off in fairly…specific circumstances, but what does it matter if you found each other?'

Somewhere across the café, Luca's voice rings

out, singing fragments of an Arabic song he learned from Layla. The universe's worst punchline.

'You want me to say I made a mistake?' I ask. 'Because I can't. I have to think of him.' I nod at Luca, who's now building a tower taller than his new friend's. 'He needs stability. I can't bring someone in and out of his life for my own benefit.' It's a flimsy excuse and he pounces on it before I can retract it.

Giuseppe leans in, his voice dropping. 'Stop talking about her like she's a flight risk. You're the one keeping her at a distance. If she wanted to fade away, she would. There's nothing in this world stopping her. But she calls every night, and if you let her, she'd be here in a week. Stop pretending like fate's the villain here, Marina. It's you.'

I feel my jaw set, the old reflex to deny and defend snapping into place, but it's a weak show. Because he's right. I am the problem here, gatekeeping her from my life out of a misplaced desire for control. Not trusting the good things in my life because they've never stayed put. When I realised Francesca and I weren't a good fit, I still thought things could be cordial between us. Nothing had prepared me for the disintegration of my personal and professional life.

Then Agron passed away, right after I thought

I had found something good again—and safe. A platonic life partner and a child who has become my own.

Maybe because of all that, I've trained myself to keep everyone at arm's length while holding on tight to Luca in a bid to protect him. But what if I'm avoiding my own hurt and nothing else? Because no matter how I look at it, Giuseppe is right. Luca is fine, since Layla makes a point of speaking to him as often as she can. He misses her, sure. But she didn't vanish.

What would it even look like, to stop bracing for disappointment? To let myself want her, genuinely? The thought is terrifying. It's also the first honest one I've had about this since she left.

Giuseppe's words won't leave me, even as Luca tugs at my sleeve to show me the crooked tower he's built. He's laughing, happy, utterly certain that Layla will call tonight like she always does. I try to smile with him, but my chest tightens with the thought I've been fighting since she left.

What if the only thing standing between us isn't distance at all, but me?

CHAPTER FOURTEEN

Layla

A WHOLE DAY in the trauma ward and the only thing I want is to peel my scrubs off, put on something clean and drink tea from the chipped mug I found at the back of the supply closet that somehow reminds me of home.

Of Sicily.

That's all I'm good for today. Anything else—the art of conversation, or human interaction more advanced than 'Hold this retractor steady or you'll kill her'—feels like an Olympic event I'm not fit to compete in.

The barracks are half a kilometre from the tent hospital, a walk that would be meditative if not for the perimeter lighting that flickers, strobing the ground into sharp relief with every power surge. I pass the mess, where two field tech nurses are drinking coffee at a folding table and argue in low, accented English about generator loads.

By the time I reach my hut, my hands are shaking—too much adrenaline with nothing left to burn. The door doesn't latch unless you hip-check it, which I do. I hit the light switch, which pops the single bulb overhead.

It isn't a real room. More like a cell: cot, metal trunk, half-collapsed shelving and a wobbling plastic table I use as a desk. My laptop sits closed, charging cable a snake across the floor. With how volatile the power can be, it's best to leave it plugged in so I'm ready for my nightly calls with Luca and Marina.

I know my personal space at my previous posts wasn't any different and yet somehow the lustre has worn off, the grubbiness far more apparent. I'm not bothered by it. If I wanted something else, I know I could have it. But something is off inside me. The spark I thought guaranteed to appear with my latest transfer isn't there. I don't know how it disappeared.

No, not true. I know, but I'm too scared to say it aloud. Or even think it.

I kick off my clogs then my scrubs, rolling the top down to my waist before I remember there's a window, curtain drawn but not opaque. I'm still not used to having neighbours again—real ones, not just the ghosts of Marina's gaze and touch reminding me of desires I'd rather not remember. I tug on a tank top and pyjama pants, then sink onto the cot and press the heels of my hands to my eyes until the burst of false stars behind them is all I see. My head is too loud, and instead of settling down since I came here last month, the chaos just seems to increase with each passing day.

I need tea. It's a compulsion more than anything, a means of turning the end of the day into a ritual instead of just a pause until it all starts again. I fumble with the kettle: one of those off-brand Euro models, the kind with a plug that sparks if you wiggle it wrong. There's only powdered milk and two teabags left from the last care package.

The mug is ugly: sky-blue, cartoon cat on the side. There's a hairline crack under the rim, but as long as I drink fast it won't matter. I set it on the desk next to my laptop and log in. They'll be waiting. I always call at eight, even though it's an hour earlier there.

My fingers hover over the trackpad for too long, and when I open the screen it's a wall of new emails, most unread. I swipe them away. Click the shortcut to the video call app. Hold my breath and count to five as the connection stutters, pixelates, then finally opens a portal to Marina's apartment.

Except it isn't Marina in the frame. It's Luca, jammed so close to the webcam that his nose dominates the shot. The background is a patchwork of construction-paper animals and scrawled numbers in rainbow marker—a whole ecosystem of kindergarten art taped to the wall behind him.

'Layla!' he shouts, and the speakers fuzz out. 'Layla, I have a secret!'

I choke on the first mouthful of tea, the burn all the way to my stomach. I haven't heard him this loud in weeks. The past few calls, he's been subdued, or distracted, the way kids get when you're not in the room and your face only exists in two dimensions. Now he's beaming, every tooth showing, hair sticking up in cartoonish spikes.

'Tell me your secret,' I say, surprised at how rough my own voice sounds.

He looks over his shoulder and, for a second, the camera tilts away to show the familiar sweep of Marina's living room—the rug, the oversized plant, the glass coffee table she and I defiled in ways I'm trying not to remember, but the memories pop up unbidden. Then Luca's face is back, but this time he's brandishing a backpack so large he could fit inside it. It's blue, with dinosaurs. Brontosaurus, I think. He points at the largest one with a pride so intense it radiates through the screen.

'I started kindergarten today!' he says, as if this is news, as if we haven't been prepping for this since the day the letter came. 'Look! Mamma bought me a good-luck friend.' He unzips the bag, then brings out a squashed plush animal—a frog, eyes bulging. He grins, hugging it.

My throat tightens so suddenly it's a physical ache. The tea is useless now. My hand just holds the mug, knuckles blanching. There's a small ache in my chest, a dull and familiar pressure I've been managing for weeks. But this—missing this, his first day—is like a fresh tear, leaking salt into all the old wounds.

Marina leans into the frame, bracing her elbow on the back of the couch. She's smiling, but it's the tired kind, the one that comes at the end of a long day. 'He asked for you all morning,' she says, and her voice is softer than I expect. 'Wanted to show you the classroom tour. But it's late now, and he needs to eat.'

Luca protests, insisting he's not hungry. The next minute is a blur of negotiation—three more minutes, two, then finally a truce:

'Tomorrow, you show me your frog's favourite place in the school,' I say.

He promises, then tries to hug the screen. His face warps into a distorted fisheye when he kisses the webcam. The impulse to reach out is so strong my fingers leave condensation prints on the laptop casing.

When he's gone, Marina stays for a moment, lingering on the line. She glances down, tucks a stray lock of hair behind her ear. 'He misses you,' she says. Then, after a beat, 'We both do.'

The air in my room feels thinner, and I don't trust my voice, so it takes me several seconds of focus before I reply, 'I miss you too.'

Silence hangs between us, somehow both comfortable and brand-new. We've spent hours sitting next to each other like that, just enjoying each other's company. But there's a difference when I can't feel her presence next to me.

It's more oppressive. Disconnected.

Which is so odd because, depending on my schedule, we sometimes stay on longer, talking about our days. How things are going with the clinic and here in South Sudan. Whatever trend she's found on Instagram, or how Luca is keeping up with his French and Arabic numbers.

I love hearing it all and I love her for taking the time to tell me. I love *her*. The feeling is not lessening with the weeks I've spent away. I thought it would dull and eventually get taken over by the excitement of being here.

I'm still waiting for the fulfilment to kick in.

'Nice that you got time to spend with Giuseppe. I don't think you get out enough,' I say when she finishes telling me about her visit to the market and the impromptu coffee date.

'Yeah, I guess it was. I'm so used to seeing him as my family lawyer, it was nice to just have a normal conversation with him. Or like…as normal as can be,' Marina replied, and something in her voice grabs my attention.

'What did you guys talk about?' My eyes flick to the time, my bones getting heavier with each hour that passes. I've been on a twelve-hour shift and I know I need sleep, but I don't want to hang up. I'll see her tomorrow but letting go of her after each call is becoming an impossible challenge.

Marina huffs out a laugh, shaking her head as if remembering the conversation alone is already too much. 'I think…he believes I'm lonely now that you're gone. And I…'

I hold my breath, but instead of finishing her sentence, I hear a high-pitched squeal and then Luca comes careening back into the frame. There's a string of Italian too fast for me to understand, but I do hear the word *food* and Marina telling him to remain calm.

Luca has never been good at keeping calm when faced with food. He's as excitable as a puppy.

'Go feed the young man. You know how he gets,' I force myself to say, even though I don't want the conversation to end. 'Tomorrow, same time?'

'Yes. Unless you're needed at the hospital.'

I almost tell her that I'm always needed, but the words die in my mouth. I nod once. The call ends. The screen returns to black, my own reflection staring back at me: pale, sallow, eyes ringed with exhaustion.

I close the laptop and cradle the tea, which doesn't have any more warmth to give. The only sounds are the faint buzz of insects and the distant hum of generators. No voices. No laughter. No Luca counting in three languages. No Marina humming at the sink. Just the hollow echo of everything I'm missing.

I swallow the tea in three gulps, ignoring the bitterness, and set the mug down with more force than I mean to. The crack under the rim lengthens, spiderwebbing towards the handle. I stare at it, wondering how long before it breaks entirely.

It's just a mug, I tell myself. *Just a cup of tea.*

But the ache in my chest doesn't go away, and I know that when I sleep tonight I'll dream of a different room, a different table, a different light.

Of course, sleep eludes me. I stretch myself out on the cot, hoping to find a comfortable position to fall back asleep. But the buzzing of mosquitoes along with the relentless thoughts clamouring in my head rob me of any peace. I stare at the cracked ceiling for another ten minutes, then again after flipping the pillow and flopping back and forth on the cot pointlessly. It's too hot, mosquito net plastered to my shins with sweat, and I can't stop replaying the call.

Not the sweet part, not even the pain of seeing Luca with his dino backpack, but the moment Marina said, '*I think...he believes I'm lonely now that you're gone.*'

Why did she say it like that? Marina has always been a woman of few words, preferring action instead. Unlike myself, who could speak for hours on end and still not finish my train of thought. Sure, I asked her what she'd spoken about with him. But she didn't need to reply. She knows that. Anything she says is always because she chooses to.

Did she want me to know she's lonely? But was too proud to say it directly? That's not really like her either.

I duck my head under the pillow as if I can block out the words, but they lodge themselves in the soft part of my brain reserved for everything I don't want to feel. If Marina is lonely, what does that make me? If anything, I'm the one who tore a hole in both our lives and then left it gaping so I could prove—something. That I could succeed on my own. That I could live for the mission. That I could want her quietly from the other side of the world, and it would be enough.

It isn't enough. The days are gruelling, which

helps. There's always someone bleeding, or burning up with fever, or just waiting to yell abuse at anyone in scrubs. The distraction is total, but at night, after the chaos, I'm left with a hollowed-out feeling that even the strongest tea can't fill.

I lie there for hours, wrestling with the question that's been nipping at my ankles since the day I left Sicily, the same thing I denied when Giuseppe prised it out of Marina, the same thing my mother tried to warn me about in her kitchen: What if leaving was the mistake?

I used to know what I was chasing—a calling, a career, or the abstract idea of doing good in a world mostly spinning towards chaos. But now I spend more time wondering what I'm running away from. The echo of Marina's voice, Luca's open-armed joy, the quiet routines we built and pretended not to build. I told myself that leaving was an act of courage, but every day it feels more like an act of cowardice.

Is it really so bad to want a quiet life? I wait for the sense of betrayal to kick in, like the ghost of my mother slapping me in the face and telling me to stop being silly. But her words echo in my skull as much as Giuseppe's.

'So you don't have to honour anything because the idea you have is wrong.'

Why am I still resisting?

I'm chasing a ghost at this point. A promise

I'm hoping to fulfil, but why? Where the call for the field—for adventure—used to be now sits an empty space with jagged edges.

Am I honouring my mother's sacrifices by denying myself? By sitting here and dwelling on things, when I could be with the people who I consider my family while still using my ability to help.

I try to grab at the memories, the conviction that I'm doing the right thing. I come up empty and think myself a fool.

Before I can fight the impulse, I pick up the phone. When I swipe to open it, the first thing that comes up is my recent calls: Marina at the top, then Mum. For a long time, I just look at Marina's, my thumb hovering over the *call* button. She'd pick up instantly, I know that. But what am I supposed to tell her? The idea in my head is only forming now, and what if I can't take it back?

With the lengths we went through to get me this placement, I'm not sure they'd even let me take it back.

I don't call. Instead, I scroll through my contacts, past her name, past my mother, until I land on 'Office of Mr Nasser'. The number is still in there from the night I called to beg for my career back, back when I thought this life was all I'd ever want. I stare at it, thumb pressed so hard to the screen I can feel my pulse.

What do I even want now? The question knocks around my skull, a sore tooth I keep poking just to see if it'll hurt. I press the heel of my palm to my forehead and squeeze my eyes shut.

For the last weeks, I've told myself that being here is enough. That it's what I fought for, what I torched everything else to get. That every day I spent at the clinic in Sicily was just a way station, not a destination. But sitting here, in a room that isn't a home, drinking tea that tastes like disappointment, I can't shake the thought that I made a mistake.

'You're an idiot,' I say to the empty room, to the walls, to the tiny lizard perched on the windowsill. 'Just call. Just…do something.'

I call Nasser.

The phone rings, and rings, and rings. I let it echo, each pulse a metronome for the heartbeat in my throat. I don't know what I'll say if he answers. Maybe I'll ask if they can reassign me. Maybe I'll invent a reason to transfer back, some loophole or emergency. Maybe I'll just listen to his voice and hang up, because sometimes that's all I can do.

I stare at the crack in the mug. My other hand shakes a little, but I let it. I let the uncertainty in, and for the first time in weeks, it doesn't feel like a defeat.

As the phone continues to ring, I steady my breath and let the determination take over.

I'm not done with Sicily. Not by a long shot.

CHAPTER FIFTEEN

Marina

THERE ARE GROOVES in the carpet from my pacing. A fresh loop worn between the living room and the edge of the kitchen. If someone dropped luminol in here, the outline of my anxiety would glow brighter than the cheap overhead lamp. The rest of the room is dim, early autumn dusk casting everything in bruised shadows.

I try not to look at the clock, but of course I do. Every three seconds, at a minimum. I haven't managed to focus on anything—my work laptop sits open to the same document as two hours ago, some reports due to the government to keep them informed of the work we're doing here.

The only thing getting done here is a marathon rehearsal of what I'll say when Layla calls.

We've spoken every day since her departure, but ever since I told her I'm lonely—through Giuseppe's words rather than mine because I'm a coward—except for the last two. Layla said she'd be out of mobile range, making it impossible to connect, but that we'd see each other today.

She hasn't called yet, the usual time lapsing, and as I walk around, steps muffled by the fluffy carpet, I almost lose my nerve. I have to tell her how I feel. That I want her to be here with me—with Luca. Make this a family.

The coffee in my mug is cold, bitter enough to sting the inside of my mouth. I drink it anyway. It gives my hands something to do when I'm not picking at the ring on my finger, or raking my nails over my scalp, or chewing the inside of my cheek until it's raw.

Tonight is the night. I'm sure of it. Tonight is the night I tell her everything. Not the half-truths we've been trading for weeks, not the deflections, not the endless dance around what we really want. I'll say it, straight out. *Please come home.* Not for Luca. Not for the paperwork or the show, but for me.

For us.

I pace and rehearse and fail.

I stop in front of the window and stare out at the street, blank and wet and empty, except for the orange glare of the streetlamp that sometimes flickers when it gets too rainy.

'Come home. Please,' I try again, letting the words fall out just above a whisper. My hand is white-knuckled on the mug. 'I love you and I want you here. For real.'

My pulse is thunder in my ears.

I grab my phone. The screen lights up, and even though I've checked it a hundred times in the last ten minutes, time still hasn't advanced. She's usually the one to call, but maybe she's waiting for me to do it this time. Or maybe she's running late and can't reach me.

I hover my finger over the call button, then pace another lap of the flat, then hover again. I want to throw the phone onto the couch and hide, but I know if I don't do it now, I'll lose my nerve forever.

I squeeze my eyes shut. 'You have to call her, you idiot,' I mutter.

But before I can, the doorbell rings.

My body snaps rigid, every muscle firing in some vestigial memory of threat. I look at my phone, then twist around to look at the landline sitting on its little pedestal on the wall. Is there an emergency? It wouldn't be the first time I get called away at stupid o'clock; it comes with the territory. But my heart speeds up, thinking of all the things I want to say and swallowing them down for another day.

But then the ring of the doorbell is followed by a slow, deliberate knock—three times, evenly spaced. That's not the urgent knock of someone in urgent need of medical care.

My heart trips in my chest.

Nobody comes by unannounced. Not in such a calm manner. I glance at the time—half past nine—and then at the street. No cars, no pedestrians, just the pulse of the lamp and the line of rain snaking down the sidewalk.

I walk to the door, every instinct bracing for the worst, and press my eye to the peephole. For a long second, I don't see anything. Then movement: a shadow, someone smallish, the blur of a dark jacket and a suitcase handle. My brain refuses to make sense of it, and then the pieces click into place and I stagger back, mouth gone bone-dry.

Layla?

I unlock the door. My hands are shaking so hard I can barely manage the deadbolt. I pull the door open and just stand there, numb, staring at her like I've conjured her out of the cold night air.

She looks exhausted. Not just physically, but all the way through, like someone who has been burning both ends of a very short candle for a very long time. Her hair is pulled back in a messy bun, wisps sticking to her temples in the rain.

She doesn't say anything. Neither do I.

Layla stands there for a beat, then two, the rain beading on her jacket and dripping onto the mat.

She sets the bag down with a careful thud, and the sound feels final in a way that nothing else has in months.

I finally find my voice, though it comes out strangled. 'You came back.'

Layla's mouth curves, a small smile that hits me squarely in the chest with its familiarity. 'I needed to see you,' she says, and then what happens next is a blur of colour and motion and breath.

Layla lands in my arms and I press her tight to me. Our faces come together, mouths hovering for a hesitant second before they come together. All my thoughts scatter and I'm done wondering what she's doing here, how she could just arrive like that.

Instead, I let myself drift into this person I know so well. The woman I love, who has stormed into my life and upended it in the best possible way.

My wife.

Our kiss deepens, her taste sweet on my tongue, and I know there and then that there's no going back for me with her. I won't ever let go of her again.

When we finally come up for air, we look at each other dazed, lips bee-stung. Silence settles between us and then we both laugh, as if this reunion was planned all along.

Layla speaks first. She clears her throat, voice

rough from travel or maybe from the effort of holding it together. 'Sorry I didn't call. I just… I realised I needed to see you to say this. So you can see my face and hear my voice when I tell you that I missed you and Luca and the clinic so much I was going out of my mind.' She gives a watery laugh that makes me want to pull her close again, but I force myself to stay where I am.

I manage to swallow around the lump in my throat. 'I didn't think—I thought you wouldn't give this up. Your work, your mission. I spent days rehearsing how to ask you to come back and now you're standing here.' My face is hot, and I can't look at her, so I stare at the wet tangle of her shoes.

Layla steps in, closing the cold night off behind her. She shakes her head, water flicking from the ends of her hair. Her hands are a little unsteady as she reaches for mine and when she finds them, she just holds on—so tightly I feel my own pulse through her fingers. 'Don't make it sound like I'm giving something up for you. And I know why you would; it's because that's how I spoke to you. But I'm not, Marina. I choose this. I choose you,' she says, and the conviction in her voice pins me to the spot. 'I want a life with you, and Luca. I want to work here. I want to build a future instead of running from one.'

I want to believe it, but I know her. I know how

she burns for her work, how she'd wither in one place if she thought it meant surrendering everything she'd built herself up to be.

'And your mum?' I ask. 'And your dad, your ghosts, everything you owe your younger self?'

Layla laughs—a sound that's frayed at the edges, but real. 'My mum says success will not love me back. And she's right.' She draws in a breath. 'I thought if I came back here I'd feel like a coward. Like I'd failed at making a difference if I didn't keep moving. But the first thing I thought when I landed in Catania was—this is where I want to be. And not because it's safe. Not because it's easy, or because my name's still on that marriage certificate, or because of some stupid decision I made far too many years ago before knowing enough about life. I want it because—' She breaks off, squeezing her eyes tight. 'Because I want you. I want us. I want all the mess and all the uncertainty and all the challenges. I thought about it for a long time and it's what I want more than a dangerous career or another war zone, or my own idea of who I'm supposed to be.'

My throat tightens again, but I manage to say, 'Me too. Idiot.'

She snorts, tension flowing out of both of us. 'You really know how to sweet-talk a girl.'

We laugh, and the sound is a release. I feel lighter than I have in months. 'I was about to call you,' I say, and it comes out more desperate than I intended. 'I was just working up the nerve. To tell you to come home. Not for—' I fumble, wanting to be exact, to say all the things I never had the courage to say aloud. 'Not for any reason other than I need you here. I want you to give us a shot. Me and you. I want to be the wife you deserve and it's pathetic how much I need you to let me try.'

Layla's face crumples a little, her brow lifting, lips twitching in a smile. 'You're ridiculous,' she says, wiping under her eye with the heel of her hand. 'You were going to call me? You know, I sat in the airport for forty-five minutes, staring at my phone and thinking, *If she isn't happy to see me, I'll just get right back on the plane*. I had an entire page of if-then statements worked out.'

A tight laugh escapes me, and now the room is so bright with us it hurts to blink. 'Layla, you could've walked in here with a second head and I would have welcomed you with open arms.'

'And you call me ridiculous?' Layla's grin is crooked, and something easy and ancient steadies between us. For the first time in weeks, maybe ever, I feel an urge to just…stop. Let things be simple. Breathe.

I brush my hand along the back of her neck and pull her to me, pressing her forehead against mine. 'If you want real,' I say, 'I can do real. I can do hard. I just can't do alone any more.' I surprise myself with it, with how true it is. How much it's been eating away at every bone in my body.

Layla closes her eyes and leans into me. 'I'm here. I promise I'm here.'

I nod, breathing her in, her hair still rain-damp and bunched up with her heady scent of flowers and…home.

Layla shifts under my grip. When she kisses me again, it's nothing like the first time. There's no urgency, no desperation, just a quiet certainty that this is where we belong. I kiss her back, slow and steady, and it feels like coming up for air after a lifetime underwater.

Afterwards, she pulls away just far enough to look me in the eyes. 'This is the beginning, okay?' she whispers. 'No more pretending.'

'No more pretending,' I echo.

We stand in the dim light, hands still joined, watching the stars grow brighter as the night progresses. I don't let go of her.

I don't ever want to let go again.

* * * * *

If you enjoyed this story, check out these other great reads from Luana DaRosa

Off-Limits Doc on Deck
Falling for the GP Next Door
Faking It with the Doctor Prince
Falling for Her Miami Rival

All available now!